A Haunting in Williamsburg

LOU KASSEM is a fourth generation daughter of the mountains of eastern Tennessee who says she has always "told stories." For years before becoming a published writer, she wrote plays, stories, and monologues for her four daughters and their friends, for schools, and for civic and church groups. "The laughter and tears associated with growing up have always fascinated me," she says. "The problems may be centuries old, but each child is different." When not writing, her favorite pastimes are reading, playing golf, traveling, and talking to young people about books and writing. Lou Kassem and her husband live in Blacksburg, Virginia. She is the author of the Avon Camelot books *Middle School Blues*, *Secret Wishes*, and *A Summer for Secrets*.

A Haunting in Williamsburg

Lou Kassem

AN AVON CAMELOT BOOK

A HAUNTING IN WILLIAMSBURG is an original publication of Avon Books. This work has never before appeared in book form.

AVON BOOKS
A division of
The Hearst Corporation
105 Madison Avenue
New York, New York 10016

First Avon Camelot Printing: May 1990

CAMELOT TRADEMARK REG. U.S. PAT. OFF. AND IN OTHER COUNTRIES, MARCA RE-GISTRADA, HECHO EN U.S.A.

Printed in the U.S.A.

OPM 10 9 8 7 6 5 4 3 2

This one is for you, Alanna Marie

Chapter One

"Jayne, we've exhausted all other possibilities."

"Be reasonable, honey."

Arms crossed, face closed, thirteen-year-old Jayne Custis stared defiantly at her parents. "I've been reasonable for five months. Now I want to go back to California where I belong."

Her father looked puzzled. "Why do you say you don't belong here, Jayne? Our family originally came from Virginia."

"They left, didn't they? Besides, I don't care about a lot of dead people."

"Martha Jayne Custis, you are being obnoxious," Mrs. Custis said. Her eyes narrowed into what Jayne called the danger zone. "I don't know what's come over you these past few months. First you crawl into a shell and don't talk to anyone. Now you're acting like a spoiled brat."

"Is that why you're sending me to live with a shrink?" Jayne shot back.

Mrs. Custis rolled her eyes heavenward, as if begging for patience. "Don't be ridiculous. Since you rejected the summer camps Mr. Howard suggested, your Aunt Liz is the only one who can help us on such short notice. That she happens to be a psychiatrist is immaterial."

"I understand Williamsburg's a very interesting place," her father said, trying to change the subject. "You might even like it."

Jayne saw this was a battle she wasn't going to win. "Okay," she shrugged. "*I'll* stay with Aunt Liz while *you* get to tour Europe."

"This isn't a pleasure trip, Jayne," Dr. Custis said. "Mr. Howard feels it's essential to field-test our language program."

"You know State Department approval is important to us," her mother said. "We've spent several years developing this system."

Looking at her parents' concerned faces, Jayne felt ashamed. "I know. I *am* being a brat. I guess I can stand a summer in Williamsburg if Aunt Liz can stand me. When do I leave?"

Four days later Jayne was scanning the crowd at Byrd Airport in Richmond, Virginia. She felt quite grown-up to be traveling alone even though it was a short flight.

"Is someone meeting you?" asked the stewardess.

"Yes, my aunt, Dr. Patricia Elizabeth Custis."

"Would you like me to page her?"

"No thanks. Here she comes." Aunt Liz was moving rapidly toward her, a welcoming smile on her long Custis face.

"Sorry I'm late," she said, giving Jayne a quick hug. "Been waiting long?"

"No, we just landed."

"Good. Let's collect your luggage and be on our way."

Jayne followed her aunt's brisk strides toward the baggage claims area. Already Aunt Liz had scored a few points. She hadn't mushed all over Jayne and she hadn't said, "My, how you've grown."

"How many years has it been since we've seen each other?" Aunt Liz asked while they waited.

"You came to Palo Alto for Christmas when I was eight. That's almost five years."

"Goodness me! I always mean to take time off but somehow I don't. I certainly meant to get up north for a visit while you were in the D.C. area. Did you get your parents off all right?"

"Yes. Their plane left forty-five minutes after mine did. At least it was supposed to. We were pretty stacked up on the runway."

"How is my absentminded baby brother? Does he still jabber at you in whichever language he's thinking in at the moment?"

Jayne giggled. Her father spoke seven languages fluently and seemed to think everyone else did. "Yes, he does."

"Then he hasn't changed much!" Aunt Liz said. "He used to drive me up the wall doing that. Oh, here comes the baggage. Which ones are yours?"

"The two dark brown ones."

Aunt Liz deftly caught the spinning luggage and handed one bag to Jayne. "Here we go. Follow me."

In a matter of minutes the bags were tossed in her aunt's car and they were driving down Interstate 64.

"Do you know very much about Williamsburg?" Aunt Liz asked.

"Not much. Dad told me a little. It's a restored Colonial city. It was once the capital of Virginia. The College of William and Mary is located there. And, more recently, Busch Gardens," Jayne recited dutifully.

"That will do for a start," Aunt Liz said, laughing. "I bought you a guide book and a Patriot's Pass. The Pass is good for the whole summer. You can see and do as much or as little as you like. Did your dad tell you that a branch of our family lived in Williamsburg in Colonial times?"

"Yes. He told me he was named after a Colonel John Custis. And that you live in his restored house."

"That's right. It's the Custis house on Duke of Gloucester Street. It was a tenement house in Colonial days."

"I didn't know they had tenements back then!" Jayne said, thinking of the shabby rows of apartments in Washington and Baltimore.

Aunt Liz laughed. "A house to rent was called a tenement in those days. John Custis never lived in my house but he owned the original. He did let our great-great-grandparents live in it for a while when they fell on hard times. It rather pleases my sense of history to live there now, though it does have its drawbacks."

"I guess so, if it's that old!"

"Age isn't the problem. The house is very modern inside. But living in Colonial Williamsburg can get hectic

4

at times. We are deluged with vistitors. Privacy can be hard to come by."

Jayne's heart did a peculiar flip-flop. Just what she needed . . . life in a fishbowl! Luckily, Aunt Liz didn't see the pained expression on her face.

"I confess I don't know exactly what girls your age like to do," Aunt Liz continued. "It's been a long time since I was thirteen. Besides, growing up on a Kansas farm we didn't have many choices."

Jayne dodged the issue of her likes and dislikes. "Dad told me about that. How did a Virginia family wind up in Kansas?"

"Itchy feet, I expect. We came from the adventurous, but poor, branch of the family tree. My grandmother entrusted me with our family saga before she died, though I've never had a chance to read all those journals. Your mom said you liked to read. You might want to look through them sometime."

"Sure," Jayne said with a definite lack of interest.

Aunt Liz gave her a quick, sharp look. "Don't care much for family history, huh?"

"Californians aren't into ancestor worship like Virginians are," Jayne retorted.

Aunt Liz threw back her head and laughed. "I'm afraid you're right about some Virginians," she said. And with that they discussed Jayne's school and Aunt Liz's work and living in the South until they drove into Williamsburg.

"You'll be able to get a better look tomorrow," Aunt Liz said as she maneuvered through the narrow, twisting streets trying to point out a few landmarks as they drove

5

by. "Right now we'd better get home. Lavina has fixed us a special dinner."

"Who's Lavina?"

Aunt Liz smiled with genuine pleasure. "She's my live-in housekeeper, secretary, and friend. I don't know how I managed before Lavina. She doesn't either."

After parking the car in a tree-shaded alley, Aunt Liz led her through a small, precisely laid out flower garden toward the back of a frame house.

"We always use the back entrance," Aunt Liz explained. "The house isn't open to the public but the gardens are. Thank heavens, the foundation does the maintenance."

A tall, regal, black lady came hurrying out the door to meet them. "Here, let me take those," she said, grabbing the bags as if they were made of tissue paper. "You sure favor your aunt, Jayne. I'm Lavina. You're mighty welcome."

"Thank you," Jayne replied. She followed her aunt into a small, thoroughly modern kitchen from which good smells wafted, making her stomach rumble.

"Any calls, Lavina?"

"Two," Lavina answered shortly. "I told them you'd call back—after dinner. It's all ready. You go wash. I'll dish up as soon as I get Jayne settled in."

"All right," Aunt Liz answered meekly.

"You still want Jayne in the blue room?"

"Yes. It's much cozier than the green one."

Lavina nodded and led Jayne up a short flight of stairs, grumbling all the way. "She hasn't had a day off in ages.

Looks to me like they could manage on their own for one day."

"Who's they?" Jayne inquired, stifling a laugh at Lavina's bossy manner.

Lavina opened a door and stood aside for Jayne to enter. "Those doctors and nurses out at the hospital!"

There was a note of pride in her voice that Jayne was quick to catch. Then she looked at her new room.

The room was small and square and painted a soft dusky blue. Each piece of furniture seemed to have been made just for this particular room. The cherry, three-quarter bed had a white comforter sprinkled with tiny blue flowers in the same shade of blue as the walls. A cherry dresser, a round table, and two chairs, placed in front of a multi-paned window, completed the furnishings. The evening sun sparkled through the crisp, white priscilla curtains, warming the room.

"Oh, I love it."

Lavina heaved the suitcases on the bed. "That's good. You wash up and come on down. You can unpack later."

"Do we dress for dinner?"

"Dress? Of course we do! I'm not serving my hot peanut soup to anybody in their birthday suit."

Jayne giggled. "You know what I mean, Lavina."

Lavina grinned back. "You get into something comfortable. The necessary's right next door."

Jayne changed quickly into shorts and a T-shirt. After a brief visit to the 'necessary,' she joined her aunt and Lavina in the dining room.

The dinner was a delight—from the peanut soup to the Apple Brown Betty served with real whipped cream.

"That was wonderful, Lavina," Jayne said, patting her full stomach.

Lavina beamed. "Glad you enjoyed it. I like to cook."

"Many meals like that and I'll have to go on a diet," Aunt Liz remarked.

Lavina snorted. "Hmph! You don't eat that way often enough to matter."

"Lucky for my arteries that I don't! Well, Jayne, I must return those phone calls. Would you like to go for a walk afterwards? Evenings are a good time to stroll. It isn't quite so hot and crowded."

Jayne covered her mouth to hide a yawn. "I'm awfully tired, Aunt Liz. We had to get up early to get packed and close the house. Could we do it another time?"

"Certainly. Let me get your guidebook and your Pass . . . just in case you aren't up when I leave in the morning."

"I'll help with the dishes," offered Jayne when Lavina began clearing the table.

"Not tonight, honey. You go on up and get acquainted with your room," Lavina said, smiling.

"I think I will," Jayne said around another yawn.

She climbed into bed and began to read the *Official Guidebook & Map* that Aunt Liz had given her. After a few pages the words began to blur and the book kept falling from her hands. Reaching up, she turned off her reading lamp. From somewhere below she heard the muted babble of a TV; otherwise, the house was quiet. Moonlight streamed in the funny little windowpanes. The moonbeams beckoned to her like a silver road.

Jayne got out of bed and went to the window. Suddenly she felt very lost and lonely. Except for Scout Camp, she'd never been separated from her parents. Now a whole summer stretched before her. Back home their house had sheltered many homesick Stanford freshmen. If college kids could feel lonely it must be okay for her, but the thought was small comfort.

A few people were still strolling the moonlit street below her window. The strollers were all in pairs, except for the young boy in Colonial dress who scampered down the opposite side of the street.

The boy halted abruptly and gazed up toward her window. Jayne stepped back into the shadows. When she looked out again the boy was gone.

Some exhibit sure is open late, she thought, climbing back into bed.

The Colonial boy had distracted her for a moment but the lonely feeling came back stronger than ever. Even with Aunt Liz downstairs she felt abandoned. Just as she was drifting, she heard someone humming a plaintive tune.

"Someone feels as sad as I do," she murmured into her pillow.

Chapter Two

Jayne came downstairs just as her aunt was preparing to leave. "Sorry I'm late. I overslept."

"There was no need to hurry. You have all day," Aunt Liz said, smiling at Jayne's tousled appearance.

"I—I thought you'd want to give me my schedule or something."

"Schedule? No, I didn't have anything planned. I thought you'd like to take your guidebook and get acquainted on your own. Lavina will be here all day. I'll be back around six. Dinner's at seven. Is that okay with you?"

"Oh . . . Sure."

Dr. Custis took the last sip of her coffee and grabbed her briefcase. "See you tonight then," she said as she went out the back door.

"What you want for breakfast, honey? Ham and eggs? Hotcakes? Some sticky buns?"

"Just juice and cereal, I guess, Lavina."

"That's not much breakfast for a growing girl," Lavina grumbled.

"All right," Jayne said meekly. "Fix me what Aunt Liz had."

"That's what she had!" Lavina said, shaking her head in frustration. "I keep telling her she needs fuel for her long day but she doesn't listen."

"What do you eat, Lavina?" Jayne asked, trying to keep from laughing.

"Ham, eggs, grits, hot biscuits. Food like that'll see me through till supper. I don't eat much in the heat of the day. Makes me sleepy."

"Have you had breakfast yet?"

"Nope. Had to fix that little bite for Doctor or she wouldn't have eaten anything."

"Then make breakfast for two," Jayne said. Suddenly she was hungry. For food and information. Maybe she could find out from Lavina just what was going on—what Aunt Liz expected from her. Better to be prepared than surprised.

In a very short time Jayne was eating her way through crisp, salty ham, sunny yellow eggs, biscuits dripping with butter, and a bowl of hot white grits. Every bite was delicious. She told Lavina so.

Lavina beamed. "Now you're all set to go."

"Where?"

"Why, anywhere you want. Don't you want to see how it used to be? How your folks started out?"

"Oh, sure. But then what? What does Aunt Liz have planned?"

"I don't know," Lavina answered, her smooth brow

12

wrinkling in puzzlement. "Is there something you want special to do?"

"No." Jayne sighed. She could see she wasn't getting through to Lavina. "I mean what classes or lessons does Aunt Liz have me signed up for? You know, pottery, dance, nature hikes, photography . . . stuff like that."

"I don't know of anything like that," Lavina replied. " 'Course, if you want it, I'm sure the Doctor can find some of those things for you. You just tell her tonight, hear?"

"I don't want it! It's just what everyone does these days—all these planned programs and camps and stuff."

Lavina grinned. "I expect Doctor thought you were tired of all that. Now, scoot! I have work to do."

Jayne scooted upstairs to the shower. She came back downstairs armed with her guidebook, her camera, and her Patriot's Pass. "Am I dressed properly?"

"You look fine to me. There's no proper way to dress here except cool. Believe me, you'll see everything."

"I'm off then."

"I'll have a fruit salad waiting for lunch."

"Ugh! How can you even think of food after that huge breakfast?"

"Easy. You'll see. Here, take a key. We have to keep the door locked or folks will walk right in."

Jayne pocketed the key and set off.

The backyard was dotted with wooden, white-painted structures of various sizes. From her readings, Jayne knew these were the old kitchens, the smokehouse, and the necessary, as the outdoor toilets were called. The neat gardens she'd already seen the night before.

13

Passing by the boarded-up well house, Jayne circled to the front and examined the outside of her own dwelling. A double row of steps led up to a tiny stoop before the unused front entrance. Two broad-based chimneys anchored each side of the steep shingled roof. Five dormer windows poked through the cedar shakes. The farthest window was hers.

As she was looking up, a shadow crossed her window. Jayne smiled. Lavina must be checking to see if she'd made her bed. Well, she had! Neatly, too.

Happy that she'd done something right, Jayne consulted her guidebook. If she went left she'd be heading toward the new part of town, Merchant's Square, while toward the right was most of the Historic District, anchored by the stately brick Capitol.

She chose the Historic route. Allow one hour down and one hour back, she decided. The rest could wait until the afternoon.

Duke of Gloucester Street was closed to car traffic so people spilled over into the street, rushing frantically from one exhibit building to the other. Babies in strollers, young kids, teens, middle-aged and elderly roamed the area armed with guidebooks and maps.

Jayne ambled along the tree-lined walks snapping pictures of the ox-drawn carts and the horse-drawn carriages just as the other tourists were doing. It was almost as much fun watching the people as it was looking at the way things were in the Colonial days.

People act like this is real, Jayne thought wryly, not just recreated.

Yet, in spite of her cynical attitude, she was drawn

into the Colonial spirit as she paused to listen to the Eighteenth-century music being played at the Music Shop.

The musician, clad in a loose white blouse, pants that came just below his knees, white stockings, and buckled shoes, played tunes on the fiddle, the hammer dulcimer, and the harpsichord. The last tune he played sounded vaguely familiar to Jayne.

"What was the name of that last one?" she asked.

" 'Maiden's Lament' is the old name," the man replied. "You might have heard the modern version, 'Lavender Blue.' "

Jayne nodded and smiled her thanks. The first time she'd ever heard that tune was last night. Either Aunt Liz or Lavina had been humming it just before she fell asleep.

When she stepped out of the Music Shop onto the street her vision blurred. Just for a second, everything changed . . . the trees were smaller, the road unpaved, the people—all of them—were dressed in Colonial costumes. Down the roadway came a horse-drawn wagon loaded with barrels and produce. Driving the team was the young boy she'd seen last night . . .

Jayne closed her eyes tightly and staggered slightly. When she opened her eyes everything was back to normal.

"Are you all right?" asked a woman with a camera and a child hanging around her neck.

"Yes, I'm fine. Must be the heat," Jayne replied, moving away quickly. Boy, that's some imagination I have, she thought. I wonder if this place affects many people the same way?

15

Tarpley's Store was the next building on the street and she went in to cool off. It fascinated her with its odd collection of smells and merchandise. She bought a scented blue candle for her room.

After the guided tour of the Capitol she came out into the bright sunlight and looked down the mile-long Duke of Gloucester Street. In spite of the tree canopy and the crowds, she could see the top of the famous Wren Building on the William and Mary campus. It was a picture postcard setting, slightly unreal, like the Playtown Village she'd had as a child.

Of everything she saw that morning, the gardens delighted her most. There were flower gardens, herb gardens, topiary gardens, and pleasure gardens with benches and fountains. Oyster-shell and brick paths wound through these delights of smell and sight. She lingered much longer than she had planned in the Ludwell-Paradise gardens and had to rush to complete her tour before lunch.

"I'll save the Governor's Palace and the George Wythe House for this afternoon," she said to herself as she joined the crowd at Bruton Parish Church, directly opposite her aunt's. "This tour won't take long."

The church and the churchyard were completely enclosed by a five-foot, round-topped, red brick wall. Jayne went inside and listened to the lecture.

She wasn't too keen on churches or architecture but the simple splendor of Bruton Parish pleased her. She could almost see the fancy-dressed English lords and ladies as they came to worship. Back then, according to the guidebook, all officeholders were required to attend church. So much for freedom of religion, Jayne thought.

The churchyard was a different matter. It was really a graveyard, full of odd tombstones and monuments. Jayne shuddered when she looked at it. She didn't fancy tromping around on somebody's bones.

The rector, coming out of the church, noted her reluctance. "It's perfectly all right, you know," he said kindly. "Some of the tombstones are very interesting."

"There sure are a lot of them."

The rector smiled. "There are more graves than there are tombstones. It was a matter of prestige to be buried here during the Colonial era. The churchyard filled very quickly. Many spaces were used two or three times. Not to worry, these souls are resting in peace now. You'll not disturb them."

Not wishing to appear wimpy, Jayne stepped into the graveyard. She'd gone only a few paces when her vision blurred again and the monuments began to thin out and shift places. An incredible feeling of danger swept over her, making the hairs on her arms stand at attention. Every nerve in her body screamed, *"Run."*

Jayne ran out of the churchyard and across the street, not stopping until she reached the back door of the Custis house. She jiggled the door twice before remembering she had a key.

A light lunch and Lavina's company calmed her, and afterwards she went back out to explore again. It was fun being on her own. For a little while she forgot her modern problems and slipped back into an earlier, slower-paced age.

By the time she sat down to dinner she was exhausted. Her legs ached from walking and her mind was saturated with the sights and sounds of an age gone by. It was difficult to come back to the twentieth century.

Aunt Liz noted her condition. "You look exhausted, Jayne. You shouldn't try to do it all in one day. You have the entire summer."

"I know. It's just that once I got started I couldn't stop. One thing leads to another."

Aunt Liz smiled. "I'm glad you're enjoying it. But I think you'd better have an early bedtime tonight or Lavina and I will have to carry you upstairs."

Jayne sat up straight in her chair. "I'm fine now. I have my second wind."

By ten o'clock she was ready to give in. Her eyes refused to focus on the TV. "I think I *will* go upstairs and read for a while," she said.

"Don't read too long," Dr. Custis advised.

" 'Night, Jayne," Lavina said.

Jayne stumbled upstairs and fell into bed. She was asleep in seconds.

Much later, she awoke; the house had a sleeping silence about it. Her room was bathed in eerie moonlight.

Jayne blinked fretfully.

Someone sniffed.

"Who's there?" Jayne demanded, sitting up. "Who's crying?"

Something moved in the shadowy corner.

A feeling of intense cold swept over Jayne. "W-w-who's the-there?"

18

The moonbeams coalesced into a figure of a young woman. She was dressed much like the hostesses Jayne had seen that morning, In a long skirt, tight bodice, and white dust cap. Her sad face looked vaguely familiar.

Before Jayne could place the face, the girl melted back into the moonlight.

I must be dreaming, Jayne thought when her mind unfroze.

The weeping had stopped. Nevertheless, it was some time before Jayne closed her eyes again.

Chapter Three

" 'Morning, Jayne. Did you sleep well?" Lavina asked as Jayne came into the sunlit kitchen.

"Like a baby," Jayne said, deciding not to mention her weird dream. "Has Aunt Liz left already?"

"She had to go early. One of her patients kept the night shift busy. Doctor left before seven . . . without her breakfast."

Jayne grinned. Lavina was acting like her mom did when she skipped breakfast before school. "I expect Aunt Liz will get something to eat if she gets hungry."

Lavina snorted. "Hah! A cup o' coffee, maybe. What do you want to eat?"

"Scrambled eggs?"

"Sounds good to me," Lavina said, brightening. "You put the toast on and I'll fix the eggs."

While they were eating Jayne asked, "What's wrong with that patient of Aunt Liz's?"

"Poor Miz Albriton. She's seeing things again," Lavina answered, shaking her head.

"What kinds of things? Little green men? Monsters?"

Lavina sighed. "No, she sees dead people. Last night it was her dead husband and his first wife. They were in Miz Albriton's bed and wouldn't get out."

Jayne giggled. "I guess three in a bed is a crowd."

"It's not funny, Jayne. Miz Albriton broke a glass and cut her mattress all to pieces. Most of the time she's a harmless little old lady, but you never can tell when she'll go off."

All this talk of seeing things made Jayne nervous, especially after her dream. She pushed hastily away from the table. "Great eggs, Lavina. Aunt Liz doesn't know what she's missing."

"Why don't you tell her? Maybe she'll listen to you. She sure doesn't to me. Well, what do you have planned for today?"

"I haven't nearly finished exploring. I'm off to see the rest of Williamsburg. Uh, by the way, Lavina, which exhibits use kids about my age?"

Lavina frowned. "What do you mean, honey?"

"You know, kids dressed in Colonial garb. A boy my age or maybe younger. I saw him run into the churchyard the other night."

"Must have been some tourist dressed up, honey. All the young folks buy those tricorn hats. You have to be eighteen to work in the Historic District."

"Oh. Well, I'd better get a move on if I want to see everything I've planned," Jayne said.

Again she spent all day exploring. The more she learned, the more she wanted to know. She talked with the hostesses, the tour guides, the gardeners, and even

22

the archeology students who were excavating an old site. She kept her eyes peeled for the young boy but never saw him. Everyone told her the same thing Lavina had— you had to be eighteen to work in Colonial Williamsburg.

For the next few days Colonial Williamsburg was her chief topic of conversation at the dinner table.

"I thought you didn't like history, Jayne," Aunt Liz teased.

"Usually, I don't. History is dull and dry. This is different. It's alive. Real."

"Not real, Jayne, reconstructed or restored. Granted, it's being done as closely as possible to what really existed but it isn't a step back in time. That's impossible," Aunt Liz cautioned.

Uh-oh, thought Jayne, that's the shrink talking. Better cool it. "Sure," she said aloud, "I know it isn't real but it makes history more interesting if you can see how it was instead of memorizing dates and junk."

"You must have seen about everything by now," Lavina said with a laugh.

"No, I haven't! I've still got lots to see."

"Maybe you should take it in smaller doses. It's getting very hot for all the walking you're doing," suggested Aunt Liz.

"I don't mind the heat."

"Lavina said you mentioned some classes. We can look into them. You might meet some people your age."

"No thanks, Aunt Liz. What I'd really like is to find the library. I want to catch up on my reading."

"There's a fairly new one located two blocks from Merchant's Square on the corner of Scotland and Boundary Streets."

"Great. Thanks."

"Tell her your surprise," Lavina urged.

"I thought we'd go to Busch Gardens on Sunday," Aunt Liz said. "And since it's Lavina's day off, we can have dinner at Christiana Campbell's Tavern."

Jayne felt a stab of guilt. Her aunt was trying very hard to please her. "You don't have to take me to Busch Gardens, Aunt Liz. I don't need to be entertained."

"Nonsense! I'd love to go myself. I haven't been there since it first opened. Just don't expect me to ride that roller coaster with you."

"It'll do her good to get away," Lavina said. "You take her up on it, Jayne."

"Okay. It's a deal. I'm not too big on roller coasters either. Heights make me dizzy."

Later, Jayne was preparing for bed when Aunt Liz called her to the phone. "Hurry, Jayne. It's your mother."

Jayne nearly broke her neck getting down the stairs. "Hi, Mom," she shouted. "How's Paris?"

"Don't shout, Jayne. I can hear you very well. Paris is fine . . . what little I've seen. We've spent most of our time in the embassy or on military bases."

"How's Dad?"

"Fine. He's a little exasperated with all the red tape. Mr. Howard wants us in another meeting at seven this morning. That's why we're up so early. How are you doing?"

"Great. Just great. Williamsburg is neat."

"And your Aunt Liz?"

"She's neat, too. We're going to Busch Gardens on Sunday. Then she's taking me to Christiana Campbell's for dinner. It's Lavina's day off."

"How's Lavina?"

"She's fine. She's a nice lady. A good cook, too."

"Have you made any new friends?"

"Gosh, Mom, I haven't been here a week yet. I'm just learning my way around."

Mrs. Custis laughed. "Just don't spend all summer with your nose in a book. A growing girl needs exercise."

"I'm getting plenty of exercise, Mom."

"Good. I don't want you to become a hermit. I'd better go now. This is costing a fortune. Remember, Aunt Liz has our itinerary if you need us. Have a good time at Busch Gardens. I miss you."

"I miss you, too, Mom. Say hi to Dad."

Jayne held the receiver long after the connection was broken. She knew her parents were worried about her. She'd really gone into her shell the last few months at Stuart Hill. But becoming a hermit hadn't been her idea. What choice had she had? No one in the whole school would even talk to her.

Aunt Liz came in quietly. "Is everything all right?"

Jayne squared her shoulders and pasted a smile on her face. "Oh, sure. Everything's fine."

"Next time you can use the upstairs phone," Aunt Liz reminded her. "It's quicker and it might save you some broken bones."

Jayne flushed. "I forgot. I'll remember next time. Good night, Aunt Liz."

25

"Good night. Sleep well. . . . And Jayne, don't fret. The summer will pass very quickly."

"Sure it will." She trudged back upstairs feeling really low. Yes, the summer would pass. But would things ever be the same again?

Jayne finally drifted into a restless sleep. She awoke during the night feeling dreadfully cold. She sat up, scrabbling for her comforter at the foot of the bed.

The girl she had seen before stood by the window, watching her.

"W-who are you?" Jayne whispered.

"A selfish coward."

Jayne jerked her comforter over her head and lay trembling underneath. This was no dream. There really was a ghost in the house. The more she thought about it the more curious and less frightened Jayne became. Who was she? Why did she say she was a selfish coward? What did she want? Finally, Jayne poked her head out from under the covers, curiosity winning out over her fear.

The girl was gone.

Disappointed, Jayne sank back on her pillow. How was she supposed to find out anything if the girl kept popping in and out like a jack-in-the-box? One thing for sure, she couldn't ask Aunt Liz or Lavina any direct questions! They certainly didn't act as if they'd seen any ghost. She would have to be very, very careful. . . .

Chapter Four

Rain clattered against the little windowpanes. Thunder rumbled and crashed, shaking the house.

Jayne opened one eye, saw a streak of lightning, and scrunched under her covers. Rain and thunder didn't bother her but lightning always scared her silly. How was she supposed to get any rest with storms and visitors invading her room? She tried to go back to sleep but her full bladder forced her out of bed.

Back in her room, she put on her jeans and eyed the stack of books by her bedside. She'd finished all of them. Now what was she going to do for reading material? She stomped downstairs in a thoroughly grumpy mood.

Tantalizing smells wafted from the kitchen.

"What's cooking?" she asked Lavina by way of greeting.

Lavina turned from the stove and grinned at Jayne's scowling face. " 'Morning, Jayne. I figured the smell of sticky buns would get you up."

"They sure do smell good," Jayne conceded.

"Taste good, too. Pour yourself a glass of milk. They're about ready."

Jayne ate three buns and felt better.

Lavina busied herself around the kitchen, not talking, while Jayne ate.

Jayne debated over a fourth bun but pushed her plate away. "Those were great, Lavina."

"You're fun to cook for. Not like Doctor. She always worries about filling up her arteries or something."

"All I worry about is filling out my bra." Jayne sighed, looking at her almost flat chest.

Lavina chuckled. "It'll happen, Don't worry."

Jayne shrugged. "That's the least of my worries. Do you think it'll rain all day?"

"I expect so. When it comes from the east it usually does."

"What are you going to do today?"

"Before I log Doctor's notes into the computer I'm going to do some baking. Want to help?"

"Sure. But I don't know much about cooking. Mom's not into that scene. I'd like to learn though."

"Wash your hands and grab an apron! We'll bake up a storm."

"We already have a storm," Jayne pointed out. "Could we bake up some sun?"

"We can try," Lavina said, flashing her wide, white smile.

"I'll be right back. Just let me make up my bed."

When Jayne returned Lavina had everything lined up on the counters. "I'm ready," Jayne said. "You want to check out my room now or later?"

Lavina looked puzzled. "I don't check up on you."

Jayne knew in a flash who had been at the window—and it wasn't Lavina. She forced a smile and told a white lie. "Mom usually checks my room. I thought you did, too."

"Not me," Lavina replied. "It's your bed. You have to sleep in it. Let's get started."

They baked all morning, first two cherry pies and then several batches of cookies.

When a vicious crack of lightning made both of them jump, Jayne saw a way to find out something about her night visitor. "Br-r-r," she said. "Thunderstorms are spooky. Now's a great time for a ghost story. Do you know any, Lavina?"

"Ghosts or stories?"

"Either one. Williamsburg seems like a perfect place for ghosts."

"I reckon you're right. Most of the old plantations claim to be haunted."

"Really? How about this house? Do we have a ghost?"

Lavina laughed and shook her head. "Never heard of one. Doctor wouldn't allow such talk anyway."

"Why?"

"Doctor's what you might call a real Ghostbuster. Her job's to get rid of such things in people's minds."

"Oh. . . . Do you think people who see ghosts are crazy?"

Lavina set the timer for the last batch of cookies. "Most likely. Or, as my granny would say, 'a little tetched in they haid.' "

Jayne changed the subject quickly. She'd just have to

find out who the girl was without letting Lavina or Aunt Liz suspect what she was doing. She certainly didn't want to visit her aunt at the hospital . . . at least not as a patient.

It was still raining after they ate lunch and cleaned the kitchen. "I think I'll go read for a while," Jayne said casually. "Do you know where Aunt Liz keeps the family journals?"

"They're in the glass bookcase in Doctor's office. You be careful with them. They're very old."

"I will," Jayne promised.

She found the seven various-sized and -colored volumes right where Lavina said. The first book was dated 1759–1791. The book seemed to tingle in her hand as she removed it from the shelf. A curious feeling of excitement welled up inside of her as she carried the volume upstairs and settled down in front of the window. Jayne had never felt so interested in family history before. Why now, she wondered as she began to read.

Three Springs, Virginia Colony
I, Elizabeth Mary Sutton, wed Nathaniel Edward Custis on April 10, 1759, at my home, Briarwoods. We arrived in Three Springs on April 30, 1759. This is an accounting of our family . . .

The ornate, brownish script with the strangely spelled words was difficult to read, but Jayne persisted. Sometimes she had to guess at the words or meanings. Elizabeth Custis' journal was almost like a diary, except she had recorded only the highlights of her marriage. Little by little the story unfolded:

Three Springs was a small holding, compared to Elizabeth's former home of Briarwood. The estate was also deeply in debt due to the spendthrift ways of Alfred Custis, Nathaniel's father. Elizabeth and Nathaniel were struggling to keep the estate afloat. They managed to hold on through the births of six children: James in 1760, Mathew in 1761, Ann in 1762 (died at two weeks), William in 1763, Sally in 1764, and Jeremiah in 1765. Nathaniel's father died in 1766. His debts to the Crown and others were called due. Three Springs had to be sold. For two years the Custis family stayed on as caretakers until Malcolm Whitney, the new owner, arrived from England.

Through the generous graces of Nathaniel's distant cousin, Colonel John Custis, the family moved to Williamsburg. Col. John let the family live in one of his houses and gave Nathaniel work on his plantation. Even so, it was difficult to make ends meet. Elizabeth, in addition to her family duties, became a seamstress. Each son, as soon as he was old enough, took odd jobs outside the family . . .

Jayne leaned back in her chair and rubbed her eyes. This was tough going! She stood and stretched. So far, while the journal was interesting, she hadn't found out anything about her ghost.

Seeing that the rain had stopped, she marked her place in the journal and raced downstairs. "I'm going to the library," she called to Lavina. "Back shortly."

She splashed her way through the puddles on the cobblestone street. A leftover gust of wind shook raindrops on her head, making her hair curl even tighter. She didn't care. No one in Williamsburg knew her or cared how she looked.

The library was easy to locate. Jayne ran up the steps and pushed on the door before she saw the CLOSED FRIDAY sign. Disappointed, she made note of the library hours and started back down the sidewalk.

A cute blond guy was parking his bicycle along the brick wall. In spite of her recent resolution never to help any male ever again, Jayne said, "The library's closed," as she passed him.

The guy ignored her and went up to the door.

Jayne watched as he repeated her actions. "See? It's closed to you, too, Mr. Cool," she said, walking away.

Back at Merchant's Square, she stopped in Scribner's Bookstore for a paperback to tide her over until tomorrow. Upstairs in the YA section she pored over the selections and finally chose a book. Going back downstairs she met Mr. Cool coming up.

He smiled at her, a wide, friendly grin that made his blue eyes twinkle.

Jayne paid him back by ignoring him. But she was suddenly very conscious of her bedraggled appearance.

"Will that be all?" asked the salesclerk.

"Yes, thanks," Jayne said, watching a group of girls her age laughing and talking as they trooped upstairs. An ache of loneliness swept over her. It seemed a lifetime since she'd been a part of such a group.

As she came out of Scribner's, time flip-flopped again

and she was once again in Colonial times. Horses and carriages filled the muddy streets. A group of bewigged men clustered on one corner, talking and gesturing. A hawk-nosed young man approached the group, smiling a greeting. The men turned their backs and closed ranks . . .

"How rude!" Jayne said aloud.

Laughter jolted her back to the present. The girls from the bookstore were standing on the walk looking at her. Jayne blushed furiously and hurried away. The book in her hand was no longer of interest. She felt impelled to get back and read more of the journals.

"Lavina tells me you've been reading the family saga all afternoon," Aunt Liz said at dinner. "How is it?"

"It's pretty tough to read that first journal. The writing and spelling are funny. Funny-strange, I mean."

Aunt Liz laughed. "From what my grandmother told me, there are some strange characters in our family. Have you come upon those yet?"

"No, everyone seems pretty ordinary so far. I mean ordinary for then."

"Keep reading. Every family has a few skeletons hanging on their family tree," Aunt Liz said, "though most families try to hide them. Everyone seems to prefer thinking that all his ancestors were descended from royalty, great patriots, or wealthy gentry."

"I've already found that our family wasn't wealthy."

"I think you'll find worse than that. My grandmother said there was a traitor in our past somewhere," Aunt Liz said. "Every time she mentioned it, my father blew a fuse. He was very family-proud. He used to boast of being related by marriage to Martha Custis Washington."

"But you won't mind if I find a skeleton or two?"

"Of course not! Those people are long dead, buried and forgotten. The past can't hurt us. It's the present that matters," Aunt Liz said firmly.

Chapter Five

Jayne paused with her hand on the doorknob. She looked at Lavina with disbelief. "Clean my room? Why? It isn't dirty. I've only been here a week."

"We always clean on Saturday. Doctor says you're responsible for your room."

Jayne glanced at the clock. It was nine-forty-five. She had wanted to be at the library by ten. "Okay. What do I do?" she asked grumpily.

"First you change your sheets. Bring your dirty laundry down to the laundry room. Then you vacuum and dust," Lavina instructed patiently.

"I want to be at the library when it opens."

"The books will still be there when you finish. Taking care of your own quarters isn't too much to ask, is it?"

Jayne meekly went upstairs. She knew Lavina must think she was a bad-mannered, lazy brat. As a penance she cleaned her room until it sparkled.

"I'm finished. Anything else?" she yelled at Lavina over the noise of the vacuum cleaner.

Lavina cut off the machine. "Doctor said remind you to write your folks."

"I will. Where is Aunt Liz? I didn't think she worked on Saturdays."

"She's out buying groceries. Doctor works even on her day off."

"Why does she work so hard, Lavina? Already twice this week she's gone back to the hospital after dinner."

"Because she cares more than the others do about their patients," Lavina answered flatly.

"Or maybe she's like my dad and is just a workaholic," Jayne said, making a face.

Drawing herself up to her full height, Lavina said, "I don't know about your daddy. But I do know about Dr. Custis. She works because she cares! I was her head nurse before I retired. So don't you go faultin' Dr. Custis."

"Oh." Jayne felt the blood rushing to her face. "Uh—er—well, I'd better go. I'll be back at lunchtime."

Lavina nodded and turned on the vacuum again.

Jayne fled. Her thoughts flew faster than her feet. That rips it! She said to herself. Foot-in-mouth disease strikes again. She hadn't meant to criticize Aunt Liz. And now Lavina's feathers had really been ruffled, too.

Jayne was out of breath when she reached the library. Filling out an application for a library card calmed her. Then, armed with her new card, she began browsing in the stacks. Not being certain what she was looking for made it difficult. She chose books on the history of Williamsburg and American ghosts, and then took Lasker's

Manual of Chess to help her brush up on her chess strategy so she'd be better competition for her father.

As she was piling up books on the edge of a table, she saw Mr. Cool reading with absorption. Did he spend all of his time in bookstores and libraries? No way. He had an awsome tan . . .

The boy looked up.

Jayne ducked her head, picked up her books, and hurried to the Young Adult section for some pleasure reading.

"I hope you don't have far to go with these," the librarian said when Jayne came to the desk.

"Not too far," Jayne replied, stacking the books and holding them under her chin. She negotiated the library doors without difficulty. But, as she went down the walk, she fell over a bicycle. Books, bicycle, and Jayne went flying.

"Oh, m'gosh! Are you hurt?"

Jayne looked up into a pair of the bluest eyes she'd ever seen. "I—I don't think so," she said, rubbing her head where a book had fallen. "How about your bike?"

"It's okay," Mr. Cool said, helping her to her feet. "The sprocket was loose. I was fixing it. Are you sure you're okay?"

"I'm fine. Check your bike. I hope I didn't damage it."

Both spoke at once:

"I shouldn't have parked here."

"I wasn't looking where I was going."

They grinned at each other. The boy checked his bike and announced it was in good shape. Then he began helping Jayne gather her books.

"Hey, do you play chess?" he asked, handing her the Lasker book.

"My dad and I play. I'm not very good."

"I just started this spring at school. I sure like it. No one around here plays," he said wistfully.

Jayne heard herself say, "We could play sometime, if you want." She was totally amazed by her own words.

"Neat! I'd like that. Do you have a chess set?"

"Yes. Dad brought me an ivory travel set when he was in Hong Kong last year. I have it with me at Aunt Liz's," Jayne answered. She still couldn't believe this conversation.

The boy misinterpreted her look. "Oh, geez! I forgot to introduce myself. I'm Peter Smallwood."

"Jayne Custis."

The boy—Peter—was looking at her intently. "I caught the 'Jane' but not the last name. I'm reading your lips. I'm deaf. Could you spell it?"

"C-U-S-T-I-S."

"Custis. Pleased to meet you, Jane Custis," he said without a trace of shyness.

"The 'Jayne' is spelled with a *y*. J-A-Y-N-E."

"Jayne with a *y*. Got it," Peter said, smiling.

"You're good," Jayne said, awed.

"It's no big deal as long as people face me like you're doing. Do you have far to go with that load?"

"Only a few blocks."

"Put some of the books in my saddlebags. I'll walk you home."

"You don't have to do that. It isn't far."

Peter took some of the books from her arms. "It's the

38

least I can do after knocking you over. Come on, give me a couple more."

Jayne handed the books to him and he stuffed them in beside his own. "There. Which way?"

"Duke of Gloucester Street. The house across from Bruton Parish Church," Jayne replied, slowly and distinctly.

"Right in the Historic District! I wondered who lived in those houses."

"I don't live there. I'm visiting my aunt. I'm a Californian."

A look of disappointment swept over Peter's face.

"What's the matter?"

"Nothing. I just thought you might be a future classmate. I'm new here myself. Dad's been at William and Mary for a year but I've been going to Staunton's School for the Deaf. It's not easy to find new friends. Especially ones who like to read *and* play chess."

"It's not easy to find new friends *period*."

Peter nodded. "I know. I felt lost when we moved here from Florida after Mom and Dad got divorced. Then I had to go to Staunton. This year I start all over again here. Do you suppose you get used to moving after a while?"

"I guess so. People move around all the time," Jayne said. "Is your father a professor here?"

"Yep. Biology department."

"My dad's in languages and Mom's in educational development at Stanford."

"Hey, we're both TK's."

"Pardon me?"

Peter grinned. "TK's are teacher's kids. PK's are preacher's kids and MB's are military brats."

"Neat! I've never heard of TK before. I just came from a school loaded with MB's and VS's, though."

Peter frowned. "What's a VS?"

"A Virginia Snob. To be one your family must be one of the original colonists," Jayne answered. She felt a twinge of guilt after saying it. After all, her ancestors were early Virginians.

"Haven't run across any of those yet," Peter said. "They sound nasty. Should I keep a sharp eye out?"

"To be honest, I don't think there are many of them. They're an endangered species. You'll know when you meet one. Their noses are stuck up so high in the air they're in danger of drowning when it rains."

Peter roared with laughter. "That's probably why they're endangered. You paint a good picture, Jayne."

Jayne felt her face flushing. "Thanks. Here we are. We have to go around back though."

Peter followed her, still chuckling. "Sure you don't need help with these?" he asked, stacking the books in her arms.

"I can manage."

"Don't forget our chess game."

"How about Monday morning? I'm going to Busch Gardens tomorrow."

"Great. I'll drop by." Peter said, and pedaled off.

"Well, I see you found some books," Lavina said when Jayne struggled into the kitchen.

"I found more than books. I found a friend," Jayne said happily.

"I'm glad you have good news, because I have some bad," Aunt Liz said. "Our Busch Gardens trip will have to be postponed. I have to escort Dr. McNeil around Williamsburg tomorrow."

"That's okay," Jayne said quickly. "But who's this Dr. McNeil? Some bigwig?"

"He's a new doctor at Eastern. Veddy, veddy British. He's on loan to us from Queensbury General in London. He's also interested in his family's Colonial history. As the only unattached female on the staff it's my duty to show him the sights. Or so I was told."

"Maybe you should hang a sign up outside, 'Dr. Custis, Travel Guide, Tours, Lodging, and Board,'" Jayne suggested.

"Perhaps I will, if this continues," Aunt Liz said, smiling. "We can still have our dinner at Christiana Campbell's though."

"I could stay and keep Jayne company," Lavina volunteered.

"No! I'm perfectly capable of spending an afternoon alone," Jayne said testily. She hated being treated like an infant.

A pained look flitted over Lavina's face but it disappeared in a smile. "Sure you are, honey."

"I have some reading to do," Jayne said. Still smarting from the baby treatment, she flounced off to her room.

"How was the guided tour?" Jane asked when Aunt Liz came home and flopped into a chair in the living room late Sunday afternoon.

"Hot and exhausting. I think the good doctor is more

41

accustomed to walking in a cooler British clime. He certainly made no allowances for the heat. And he wanted to see everything."

"Did he like it?"

"I'm not certain. It may just be typical British reserve but I had the distinct impression he wasn't too fond of anything American," Aunt Liz replied.

"He'd better be careful. We kicked the British out once before," Jayne said, holding up the *History of Williamsburg*.

Aunt Liz chuckled. "Right you are! I'll remind him of that if he gets too stuffy. Now, let me go shower and change and we'll be off."

Dinner at Christiana Campbell's was scrumptious. Jayne ate every morsel put in front of her.

Over dessert, Aunt Liz said, "Lavina's sorry she upset you. As you've no doubt noticed, she's very protective. But she truly didn't mean to frighten you."

The forkful of cherry cobbler stopped halfway to Jayne's mouth. "Me? Afraid of Lavina? That's dumb."

"She said you ran like a rabbit when she fussed at you."

"I wasn't afraid. I was embarrassed about sticking my foot in my mouth. I'm sorry, Aunt Liz."

"I told her it was something like that. But when you didn't want her to stay with you today she was sure I was wrong."

"Geez! I only resented being treated like an infant with a baby-sitter. I didn't mean to snap at her. I'll tell her tomorrow."

"Good. Now, finish your pie or put your fork down," Aunt Liz advised, smiling.

After eating the very last crumb, Jayne asked, "How did you two get together?"

"Besides being a good friend, Lavina was my right hand at the hospital. She took early retirement when her husband retired. Unfortunately, he died quite soon after that. Lavina was devastated, lonely, and uncertain what to do with her life. Confidentially, I was very worried about her. So I asked her to come help me make some sort of order in my home office. Like Caesar, she came, she saw, and she conquered. We've been together for two years. It works well for both of us."

"I'll say."

Aunt Liz laughed. "Have you had enough to eat?"

"I'm full up to here," Jayne said, holding her hand under her nose.

"Why don't we take the long way home and walk off some of those calories? Then you'll sleep like a log."

I certainly hope so, Jayne thought. I don't want any ghosts tonight.

Chapter Six

"Jayne . . . Jayne, you got company!"

Jayne was in her room changing clothes for the third time just in case Peter actually showed up. Thinking back over their meeting, she wasn't sure Peter would come by as he'd promised. But if he did she wanted to look better than she had before. She gave her curls one last swipe with a brush and ran downstairs.

"Hi."

"Hi."

"I guess you've already met Lavina," Jayne said, remembering her manners.

Peter nodded.

"We've already introduced ourselves," Lavina replied. "You all go on about your business."

"I thought I'd take you through William and Mary in return for a game of chess," Peter said.

"Sounds like a fair exchange. Let's go. . . . or would you rather play chess first?"

"Let's tour the campus while it's cool."

"Okay. Lavina, we'll be back later," Jayne called, as she followed Peter out the door.

"Do you have a bike?" Peter asked.

"No. Not here."

"You could rent one if you wanted. The Bike Shop rents by the day, week, or month. There are lots of neat places we could ride."

The "we" decided for Jayne. "Really? That sounds great! I'll ask Aunt Liz tonight."

"I'll chain my bike to your fence, if that's okay. We'll walk today."

Peter was a good guide. As a professor's son he had access to all the buildings on campus. He managed to show Jayne most of them, ending with a flourish at Crim Dell.

"This is my favorite spot," he said as they stood on the humpback bridge and watched the ducks and goldfish swim underneath them.

"I can see why," Jayne replied, looking around the tree-shaded nook which was tucked in the middle of the busy campus. "This is neat. I wish we had something to feed the ducks."

"Maybe we could bring a picnic out here one day and give them our scraps. That's what the college kids do."

"All right! I'll bet Lavina packs a mean picnic. We could even bring the chess set."

"Speaking of chess, we'd better get back and get started. I'm meeting my dad at one for tennis."

"So that's where your great tan comes from!"

"Yep. Now that I don't swim anymore I have to do

something to keep in shape. Besides, it's good for Dad. It's the only exercise he gets, except walking to class."

"Why don't you swim anymore?"

"That's the way I lost my hearing. Two years ago I was on the Florida Sunfish team . . . training for Junior Olympics . . . when I got a really bad infection. Before we could get it under control I'd damaged both eardrums. I lost about sixty five percent of my hearing. No more water sports for me now."

"Bummer! Can't the doctors do anything?"

Peter shrugged. "I think we've tried every ear doctor in the U.S.A. So far, no luck."

"Hey, don't give up. They're making new discoveries all the time."

"I haven't given up. And, for sure, Dad hasn't. I just don't want to spend my life running from one doctor to another. Come on, let's go play our chess game."

Peter wasn't as good a chess player as he was a guide. Jayne beat him three matches in a very short time. Peter didn't seem to mind. He was sharp and eager to learn.

"How about tomorrow?" he said, rising reluctantly.

"Suits me. And I'll talk to Aunt Liz about renting a bike."

Peter grinned. "I'll put some muscle in those legs of yours. Better be prepared."

"I'm stronger than I look," Jayne retorted, smiling.

The next ten days were terrific. There had been no more cold blasts of air in her room. No sobbing. No humming. No time warps. No girl in the moonlight. And, to tell the truth, Jayne hadn't been looking for her. Exploring the present Williamsburg was much more fun than unearthing the past.

Above all, there was Peter. They spent some part of every day together exploring Williamsburg and beyond on their bikes. Peter had become a pretty fair chess player, too. He was fun to be with and easy to talk to. In short, Peter was cool.

Even Lavina thought so. One evening at dinner she said, "You two are something else! You and Peter go together like ham 'n' eggs."

Jayne turned bright red from the neck up.

"It certainly proves a pet theory of mine," Aunt Liz said. "Handicapped people should be mainstreamed, not tucked away by themselves."

"That's funny," Jayne said. "I never think of Peter as handicapped."

"Good for you!" said Aunt Liz.

Jayne thought about her aunt's theory as she watched Peter feed the remains of their lunch to the ducks at Crim Dell the next day. When he rejoined her under the trees she said, "Peter, did you want to come to Williamsburg or stay in the School for the Deaf?"

"At first I wanted to stay in Staunton and be around people handicapped like I am."

"What changed your mind?"

"One of my teachers. He said I was lucky. I had my speech, my sight, and my health. He thought I should be out in the hearing world. And the sooner I got out of Staunton the better I'd be."

"Wasn't he being kinda rough?"

"Yeah. I wanted to punch his lights out when he said

48

it the first time. But he kept nagging me worse than a parent. So I figured, why not? I can always go back if it doesn't work."

"You won't go back," Jayne said with conviction.

Peter couldn't hear the certainty in her voice but he must have seen it in her eyes. "Thanks for the vote of confidence. Come on, let's go to Baskin Robbins. My treat."

"After that I'll beat you at a game of chess . . . just to return the favor."

"You're on!" Peter began striding up the path toward their bikes. "The loser buys ice cream tomorrow."

The weather was so hot they usually played chess in Jayne's room, seated by the dormer window. Today, it seemed the game was barely underway when Peter announced he had to go.

"Dad has a court reserved for two-thirty," he explained.

"Do you have to play today? It's awfully hot."

Peter gave a wistful look at the board. " 'Fraid so. How about if I come over after dinner?"

"Suits me. It's your move."

"I know. I know," Peter said. Jayne had his king penned. I'll be back a little after eight. Okay?"

"Okay. Don't whip your dad too badly."

Peter groaned. "I wish. He has a great backhand."

Peter was as good as his word. He returned with a sunburned nose and the news that he had beaten his father in straight sets. "I'm on a roll. Let's get at it."

In a few aggressive moves he had his king free and they were evenly matched for some time.

49

Jayne had begun another strategy and it was Peter's move. She waited patiently, looking out the window at the evening strollers.

"There he is again!" she shouted, leaning closer to the window.

Peter touched her arm. "What is it?"

"That boy! I saw hm again."

"What's he doing?"

As quickly as she could, without running her words together, Jayne told him.

Peter's eyes sparkled. "It's some local kid up to mischief, I'll bet. Let's go see what he's up to."

"In the graveyard? At night? Are you crazy?"

"No, just curious. Come on, Jayne."

It was awfully hard to refuse Peter's bright blue eyes. Jayne swallowed her fear. "Okay. But you better promise to stick close to me."

"Like glue."

"Going out for a little walk," Jayne called as Peter dragged her out the door.

By mutual consent, they slowed their pace as they ambled across the street. Bruton Parish Church was dark tonight. Usually there were meetings going on or services being held.

Jayne wished something were in progress tonight. She clutched Peter's hand in an iron grip as he pushed open the wooden gate and stepped inside the churchyard.

The gray obelisks and table tombstones looked even spookier in the fading light. Shadows were everywhere in the deserted churchyard.

Jayne let out a shriek as two bats swirled and dipped above her head.

Peter couldn't hear her. He kept circling the graveyard peering behind every tombstone.

They were halfway around the enclosure when the hair on Jayne's neck rose. A chill shot down her spine. Someone was following them! She risked peering over her shoulder and stumbled over a small marker.

"Are you hurt?" Peter whispered.

"No," she replied. Then, realizing Peter couldn't see her lips in the half-light, she shook her head and scrambled up.

Peter took her hand again and resumed his search.

Jayne followed, literally on his heels. Her fear was even stronger. It was as if someone behind her was coldly furious. The hatred that threatened to envelop her was strong enough to freeze the blood in her veins. She was having a hard time breathing. Time was tilting backwards again. . . .

Jayne shook her head to clear the strange feeling.

At last, they reached the side gate leading to the Palace Green. They hadn't found a living soul.

"Well, I guess he went to ground," Peter said, chuckling.

Jayne's heart was pounding too hard for laughter. She didn't let go of Peter's hand until they were safely outside of the brick wall and under the street lamp.

"What's wrong, Jayne? You look like you've seen a ghost." Peter teased.

"S-something in there didn't like me!" Jayne gulped air and rubbed her arms to get her blood circulating again.

"Aw, Jayne, what's the matter with you? You don't believe in ghosts, do you?"

"I don't like tramping all over dead people," she said, looking over her shoulder. "The graveyard is full. Most of the graves aren't even marked. The rector said so."

Peter shrugged and said, "Okay. Let's go finish our game."

Jayne didn't need urging. She could still feel the fury flowing from the graveyard on the night air. Never, ever was she going in that cemetery again! She was still shaking when they reached the safety of her room.

"Boy, you really are spooked," Peter said. "Did I miss something? I know you're not chicken."

"I'm the biggest chicken you'll ever know," Jayne said with disgust. "I'm not even brave enough to stand up for myself."

"Just because you got spooked in a cemetery?"

"No," Jayne mumbled, hanging her head. The painful memories of Stuart Hill flooded through her.

Peter touched her arm. "What's the matter? Tell me, Jayne."

"I let Graham Stuart take credit for my essay."

"What?"

All the resentment she had held inside for months burst out. "I didn't fit in at that fancy private school from the very first day. Everyone was either from a government, military, or an old Virginia family. I was a Californian and a civilian. Believe me, Peter, it was a tight clique. For weeks no one even spoke to me. Then this guy, Graham, and I started doing our homework together in study hall. Well, I was doing most of our assignments but I didn't care. Because when Graham noticed me it was like a stamp of approval. Suddenly I had friends."

"Some friends!" Peter said when Jayne paused for breath. "Wouldn't your teachers notice after a while?"

"We didn't have the same classes or teachers. Graham was smart but lazy. Anyway, we both had to write an essay for social studies. I did mine, brought it to school, and somehow lost it. No big deal. I had a rough draft at home. I did another, handed it in, and forgot about it."

"I think I smell a skunk."

"It gets worse. Graham's teacher entered his essay in a regional contest. It won! When Mr. Sykes, our principal, read the essay in assembly and asked the first-place author to stand and take a bow, both Graham and I stood."

"Hoo-boy!"

Jayne felt the hurt and anger rising inside her once again. "We were sent to the principal's office. Just before we went in, Graham whispered, 'Let me handle this and we'll be home free.' He went into the office and said, 'I'm sorry, Mr. Sykes. It was an honest mistake. Jayne and I worked on our papers in study hall. I guess they sounded a lot alike.' "

"You let the jerk get away with that?"

"I was struck dumb. It was all I could do to breathe."

"What did Sykes say?"

A look of disgust swept over Jayne's face. "He fawned all over Graham! Said he knew that a son of one of Virginia's finest families wouldn't be dishonorable . . . junk like that. Then he said for the good of the school and our reputations we'd call it a mistake and keep it just among the three of us. He let Graham go."

53

"Not you?"

"Not me. I got chewed out for taking advantage of a fine young man's friendship. When I tried to tell him the truth he said I was a show-off and a troublemaker. He warned me to keep my mouth shut."

"Did you?"

"*I* did, but Graham didn't! He rushed right out and told everyone I'd tried to get him in trouble because he wouldn't take me to some dumb party. I wound up with no friends and a bad reputation. My mistake was in being too chicken to tell the whole school what a sleaze Graham was."

"That was your second mistake. The first was doing that jerk's homework."

"What was so terrible about that? Graham was smart. He could have done that stuff."

"That isn't the point and you know it," Peter said, shaking his head. "You can't buy friends. What did your parents say about this?"

Jayne was furious. "I didn't tell them! They wouldn't have understood any more than you do. My parents don't make mistakes. Besides, they had more important things than me on their minds."

"But . . ."

"Jayne," Aunt Liz called. "Dr. Smallwood just phoned. He wants Peter to come home right away."

"Okay," Jayne yelled, and relayed the message.

"We haven't finished our game," Peter complained.

"You'd better go," Jayne snapped, waving him away. She didn't want to talk anymore. She'd done too much already. Refusing to look at Peter, she got up and started downstairs.

Peter followed her. When he joined her at the back door, he said, "See ya tomorrow," just as if nothing had happened.

"I'm tired, Aunt Liz. I'm going on up to bed," Jayne called.

Her room felt like the inside of a freezer. Shivering, she grabbed her pajamas and went to the necessary to undress.

Once she was in bed she was warm enough but couldn't sleep. Peter's idea that she had been partly to blame gnawed at her. How could he think that? She'd certainly never looked at it that way. Or had she? Was that why she hadn't told her parents? Would they have understood? Of course not! They'd never been so lonely they'd try to buy friends. No, they would have been ashamed of her, thought she was an awful person. Peter probably thought so, too . . .

Jayne tossed and turned and still sleep wouldn't come. Finally, she turned on her light and read until she heard Aunt Liz and Lavina coming up to bed. The awful feeling that she'd lost Peter's friendship haunted her. It was a long time before the soft humming of "Maiden's Lament" lulled her to sleep.

Chapter Seven

Jayne hung around the house until eleven-thirty. Peter didn't show.

"I'm going to take my books back to the library. Tell Peter where I am when he comes by," she said to Lavina.

"Don't you want some lunch first?"

"I'm not hungry. We'll eat later."

She flung herself on her bike and pedaled off, still in a bad mood. She hadn't slept well. It was sticky and hot. Traffic was terrible. You couldn't go two feet without stopping for some of the gawking tourists who were packing the town for Monday's big Fourth of July celebration.

Even the library was full of people, yet no one she wanted to see. Mrs. Noble, her favorite librarian, wasn't at the desk. Peter wasn't in his spot. And, to make matters worse, she couldn't find any books that appealed to her. She left.

"Where do all these people come from?" Jayne fumed when she marched into the house. "Has Peter come by?"

"You're starting to sound like a townie when you fuss

about the tourists," Lavina said, laughing. "No, Peter hasn't come by yet. Sit down and have some tuna salad. You'll feel better on a full stomach."

Jayne doubted it but she ate anyway.

One of the only drawbacks in having a deaf friend was that you couldn't call each other on the telephone. So far it hadn't been much of a problem. They set times or Peter showed up around nine or, at the latest, by two o'clock.

When Peter hadn't come by two-thirty, Jayne decided to go look for him. "I'm going over to Peter's," she called to Lavina. "If we miss each other tell him I'll be at Baskin Robbins."

"I'll listen out for him," Lavina promised.

Jayne took the back streets to avoid the crowds.

Peter's house was the third small white bungalow in a string of small houses on Jamestown Road. Peter called it Faculty Row because most of the houses were occupied by William and Mary professors.

As she pulled into the postage-stamp yard, a beautiful blonde girl came out of Peter's front door.

Jayne stared, openmouthed. The girl's perfectly groomed, long blonde hair gleamed in the sunlight. Her honey-tanned figure was shown off to perfection by white short-shorts and a well-filled blue T-shirt. She has a figure that would make a monk whistle, Jayne thought enviously.

The girl stared back. "Peter isn't here," she said, walking down the sidewalk toward Jayne.

"Oh." Jayne was suddenly very conscious of her tousled hair and crumpled shorts.

"You must be the girl Peter's been hanging out with while I was away."

"I guess I am. Who are you?"

"I'm Deedee. I've been on vacation for three weeks. Thanks for keeping Peter occupied while I was gone."

Jayne had a sinking feeling in the pit of her stomach. "You're welcome . . . I guess."

Deedee smiled possessively. "Peter's a major hunk, isn't he? Everyone says we make an awesome twosome."

"Where is he?" Jayne asked, seeing Peter's bike chained to the porch. She knew he had to be around somewhere. He never went anywhere without his bike.

"I told you he isn't here," Deedee replied in an injured tone.

"Yeah, sure," Jayne said, glaring up at the house before she rode off.

"Hey, thanks again for the stand-in service," Deedee called.

Jayne didn't bother answering. The street and traffic blurred in front of her. A car honked loudly as she cut in front of it. The horn scared her. She fought to control the wobbly bike and the tears that ran down her hot cheeks.

She'd thought Peter was her friend. All along he'd just been waiting for Miss Teenage America to get back from vacation. Still, he could have come out himself and told her to bug off!

"I guess after last night he doesn't want to see my wimpy face again," Jayne muttered between sobs

Mindlessly, she rode around and around the Historic District until it was time for dinner.

After dinner she retreated to her room, pleading a headache. As soon as she walked into the room she spied the journal lying open on the table.

"I don't remember leaving that there," she said aloud, frowning. Nevertheless, she plunked down in the chair and began to read. One escape hatch was as good as another.

She read the lively accounts of Publick Times, when twice each year the General Court was in session, and people jammed into the city. There were horse races, fairs, and formal balls . . . all of which her ancestors participated in to some degree. Elizabeth was proud of her family's growing prominence and recorded each step up the social ladder.

The Custis family supported the Virginia Declaration of Rights in 1776 and were ardent advocates of American independence. Elizabeth was less enthusiastic about having James, Mathew, and William join the new American army. She was happy when Col. John refused to let her husband Nathaniel march off to war.

Jayne began reading about the war years—1776 to 1781. The journal was full of domestic matters and accounts of the two children who remained at home, Sally and Jeremiah.

Sally was being courted by several respectable suitors but as yet favored none. . . . Jeremiah itched to get into battle but had settled down as a provender for Christiana Campbell's Tavern. . . . Some well-placed families had definite Tory leanings and were to be shunned. Sally must be jealous of her favors, considering these circumstances. . . . Jeremiah was a lovable scamp who was overly fond of wealth but a conscientious worker. . . . Col. John and Nathaniel vehemently opposed moving the capital to Richmond. . . . Jeremiah was gone for long periods while gathering supplies for the Tavern from outlying farmers. . . . Sally remained hardheaded and hard-hearted toward her most respectable suitor, Wyatt Saunders. . . . General Washington was on his way to Williamsburg. Cornwallis was entrenched in Yorktown. Nathaniel said a great and final battle would be fought. . . .

The handwriting changed so abruptly Jayne thought another person had written in Elizabeth's journal! She read the lines again:

> *Our son is dead. Jeremiah, our youngest, fairest, most loving son was shot as a traitor and a spy. No matter what evidence they present, I will never believe this lie! Even were it true we would never disown our son, as some think we should. The townspeople are set against us. We are avoided by people we once called friends.*
>
> *My darling Sally has taken to her bed and refuses nourishment. It is more than grief, I fear, though she and Jeremiah were so close. The ague is sweeping through Williamsburg and I believe Sally has a bad case of it. Nathaniel is distraught. My heart is breaking but I must be strong or else we shall not survive.*

Jayne's room was icy cold. She shivered and read on:

> *October 20, 1781: We buried our Sally beside her beloved brother today. Col. John allowed us a small plot on*

his property where vandals will not desecrate their graves. The city celebrates Washington's great victory whilst we weep. We have gained our freedom and lost two of our treasures.

Elizabeth's love and sorrow came through the brief words and twisted Jayne's heart. Poor Elizabeth! Three sons away at war, a daughter dead from illness and grief, and another son shot as a traitor.

"Jeremiah was no traitor!" The words, angry and clear, broke the silence of the cold room.

Jayne jerked around. The girl stood behind her, her eyes flashing anger. "S-Sally?"

The girl inclined her head in barest acknowledgment. "You must not think this of Jeremiah! I was the guilty one. Aye, and a coward to boot. For I did not tell the truth of Jeremiah's mission. I was afraid. Jeremiah did it for me."

"Did what for you? Betrayed his country?"

"No!" Sally said, stamping her foot soundlessly. "I thought you would understand."

"Understand what? So far you haven't told me anything."

"I wish to," Sally said, contritely. "You are a kinswoman and my best hope. Will you listen?"

Jayne nodded.

Sally's eyes became misty. "I loved Colin the first time I saw him. He came to love me, too, though we saw too little of each other."

"Who's Colin? Was he a soldier?" Jayne asked, thinking she'd missed something.

"Nay. Colin was a planter's son. His plantation was near Yorktown. He came to Williamsburg often before the war, less after it began. His family were Tories. Father forbade me to see him."

"Oh, I see."

"Pappa couldn't forbid him the church! So we saw each other anyway," Sally said smugly. " 'Twas not nearly enough. Colin asked me to run away with him and marry. I sent my answer by Jeremiah. Colin was to set the place of our meeting. I promised to be here waiting. And I was."

"What happened?"

A look of extreme anguish washed over Sally's face. "I know not! Jeremiah was caught as he slipped back through the picket lines. He had a purse of English silver with him. Poor Jeremiah. So as not to betray us, he told one of his wild tales . . . saying he was one of Rawley's Runners. Of course the soldiers didn't believe him. So he broke away and made it as far as the churchyard before he was shot."

"Why didn't you tell where he'd gone?" Jayne demanded.

Sally hung her head. "At first I was overcome with grief. Then I was afraid to confirm their vile suspicions by saying he'd talked to a Tory. And, to be truthful, I was selfish. I wanted Colin to come and take me away as he promised. Mama would have locked me in my room. She wished me to wed old Wyatt Saunders. When I became ill I tried to tell the truth but Mama thought I was out of my head with fever."

"Did Colin ever come?"

Sally shook her head sadly. "My true love deserted me just as yours had done."

Jayne sat up straight in her chair. "What are you talking about? . . . Peter? He's not my true love! He was just a friend."

"You grieve for him," Sally pointed out.

Jayne blushed. "That doesn't mean I love him, for goodness sake! Things are different now."

"Not for me," Sally replied. "I cannot rest until I right the wrong I have done. Even now Jeremiah taunts me to come to the church and confess." She pointed sadly to the street below.

Jayne turned to look out the window. She saw Jeremiah standing by the churchyard gate, beckoning. Goose bumps rose on her arms.

A sharp rap on her door made her jump.

"Jayne, are you still awake?"

Jayne blinked. Was she awake? "Uh—er—yes, Aunt Liz. I've been reading."

"How's your headache?" Aunt Liz asked from the doorway. She was looking right through Sally! "This room is freezing. You must have the air conditioner turned too high."

As she came into the room to check the thermostat Sally aimed a well-placed kick at Aunt Liz's backside.

"Don't!" Jayne shouted.

Dr. Custis spun around. "Jayne, what *is* the matter with you? There's no need to shout at me. I think you should go to bed. It's after one o'clock."

"Sorry. I didn't mean to shout."

As soon as the door closed, Jayne hissed, "Why did you do that?"

"She's worse than all the others who have lived here! She's a kinswoman, yet she refuses to acknowledge me," Sally replied in a fretful voice. "I am in dire need, Jayne. Will you help me?"

"What do you want from me?"

"Set the record straight," Sally said, pointing to the open journal. "Then go tell Jeremiah that I have confessed. His spirit should not be doomed to wander this place forever."

"Why don't you tell him yourself?" Jayne asked, shivering at the thought of going into the cemetery again.

"I cannot! I died with an oath upon my lips. I swore never to leave this place until Colin came for me. I am here for all eternity. But that matters not. Jeremiah should be allowed to rest in peace."

"Why me?"

"Because you are a Custis," Sally said, giving Jayne a cold stare. "You should wish to restore the family honor."

"I—I'm afraid," Jayne said, casting her eyes downward, unable to look at Sally's pleading face.

When she finally looked up Sally was gone. Only an aura of troubled sadness filled the cold, cold room.

Chapter Eight

Jayne awoke feeling disoriented. Had she made up Sally and Jeremiah after reading the journal? No. She'd seen them before she read about them. Why hadn't Aunt Liz seen Sally? Was she, Jayne, crazy, dreaming, or just overly imaginative? Why was this happening to her? She had enough trouble without some unsettled spirits messing up her head!

She hurried downstairs, hoping for a normal, routine Saturday to put her back on track.

"'Morning, Jayne," Lavina greeted her. "I was just about to go pull you out of bed. Things are at sixes and sevens around here."

There goes my normal routine, Jayne thought. "What's up?"

"Sit and eat," Lavina said, taking a plate of scrambled eggs, bacon, and toast from the warmer. "First off, Doctor got called back to the hospital early by that new English doctor. That leaves you and me to do the cleaning *and* the shopping. I want to get it all done by two because my sister is picking me up at three. We're having a big Fourth of July reunion at the homeplace."

"The fourth isn't until Monday."

"Everybody is coming in early. We have a big family so we have lots of cooking to do," Lavina said, laughing.

"So you're leaving today instead of tomorrow?"

Lavina nodded. "Longest I've ever been gone. Won't be back till Tuesday. You'll help me get things ready, won't you?"

"Sure. I haven't got anything better to do."

"Eat up then and let's get crackin'."

When Lavina said "get crackin'" she meant it. They worked like two whirlwinds, finishing with just enough time for Lavina to get dressed and packed before three o'clock.

"Doctor will be home soon," Lavina said as she hurried out the door in response to an impatient horn. "You-all have plenty in the freezer to eat."

"Don't worry, Lavina. We'll survive. Go and have a good time at your reunion."

The horn tooted again and Lavina left.

Jayne grabbed a Coke and sank into a chair in the den. It was the first chance she'd had to collect her thoughts. The clutter in her mind refused to come together in any logical order. Peter . . . Sally . . . Jeremiah. All tumbled through her head like clothes in a clothes dryer. Before she could stop her spinning thoughts, she heard the back door open.

"Yoo hoo! Anybody home?" Aunt Liz sang out.

"In here," Jayne answered.

Aunt Liz came in looking extremely tired. "My gracious, what a day! Has Lavina left?"

"You just missed her. Could I fix you something to eat?"

"No thanks. What I need at the moment is a long shower and a short nap. I'm pooped."

"Go ahead. I'm going to the library," Jayne said, plucking a piece of reality from her spinning thoughts. "Lavina left a casserole for dinner. I'll be back in plenty of time to put it in the oven."

"Dinner? Oh, Lord! I forgot," Dr. Custis wailed. "I'm supposed to have dinner with Dr. McNeil. It wouldn't do to stand him up. He doesn't have a very high opinion of us Colonials to start with."

"You shouldn't stand him up. I'm perfectly capable of fixing my own dinner," Jayne said. "Now go catch some Z's so you'll make a good impression."

Aunt Liz laughed. "You sound just like Lavina. It must rub off. Okay, you'll get no argument from me."

Jayne finished her Coke and let herself out. She had remembered something from her conversation with Sally that could be checked. Sally had mentioned a Raleigh's Runners. Jayne was sure she'd never seen or heard of them before. So, if such a group existed, she hadn't been dreaming.

At the library she read everything she could find in the stacks and even cross-referenced Raleigh's Runners but found nothing.

Well, that tears it, she thought as she slumped toward the door. What do I do now?

"No books today, Jayne?" Mrs. Noble asked.

"No. . . . Mrs. Noble, do you have any other books on Williamsburg during the Revolutionary War other than the ones on the shelf?"

"Certainly do, Jayne. We have quite a few books in the DAR Special Collections room. It's down the hall on your right. Be very quiet. Someone is in there working."

With a sense of rising excitement, Jayne walked into the small room.

A thin-faced, hawk-nosed man was seated at one of the two tables. He looked up, smiled politely, and went back to reading one of the several books he had piled before him.

Jayne began skimming indexes. Not one book had anything about Raleigh's Runners! Finally, she selected a few books, and sat down and began flipping through them.

It was quite by accident that she came upon what she was looking for. Under the heading "Our Early Spy System," she saw a paragraph on Captain William Rawley:

Captain Rawley formed a loosely connected Eastern Shore spy network, composed of patriotic slaves, merchants, fishermen, farmers and—sometimes —children. Rawley's Runners, as they were called, reported the movements of the British Army to the American Army. These members were unknown to each other and gained passage through American lines by an identifying silver coin. (See illustration.) Captain

Rawley (3rd Regiment, South Carolina) died in the battle of Yorktown, October 9, 1781.

"I was spelling it wrong!"

"I beg your pardon?" the man said, looking at her curiously.

"Nothing. I'm sorry," Jayne said. Her mind had begun whirling again. She stared at the illustrated coin on which a coiled rattlesnake was poised to strike. In her present state, Jayne wouldn't have been surprised if it had jumped off the page and struck her.

Hastily, she pushed the book away and fled the quiet room.

"Did you find what you were looking for?" Mrs. Noble asked as Jayne rushed past.

"Yes!" Jayne replied without slowing down.

This is so confusing, Jayne thought as she made her way through the late afternoon crowds. Rawley's Runners *had* existed. If Jeremiah had been a part of this spy network he would have had a silver coin, wouldn't he? All he had to do was show it. Why hadn't he? Why did he want Sally to come to the church? Why didn't he want Jayne there? For sure, something or someone didn't!

She shivered in the steamy July heat. Try to think logically, she told herself. Pretend it's a chess game. What's your next move?

The more she thought the more confused she became. Her head was pounding.

"I must be nuts!" she said, letting herself in and going

quietly up to her room. "I'm going to sleep off this head-ache and forget the whole mess!"

Sally's plea echoed in her head: *I am in dire need. Will you help me?*

"*No!*" Jayne said aloud. She covered her head with her pillow and, finally, slept.

Chapter Nine

"Jayne."

"What?" Jayne yelled right into her aunt's face.

"My goodness! I didn't mean to scare you."

"That's okay," Jayne replied, trying to keep her voice steady. Her heart was pounding like a jackhammer.

"Dr. McNeil and I are leaving now. I'm not sure what time we'll be back. We're taking the ferry over to Nick's. You aren't afraid to stay here alone, are you?"

"Of course not!" Jayne said with as much indignation as she could muster.

Aunt Liz smiled. "I thought not. I'll see you in the morning then. Don't wait up for me."

"Okay. Hey, you look awfully nice tonight. Have fun."

"Thanks. I'm sure we will. Dr. McNeil is really a very interesting man."

Jayne waited until she heard the back door close and then went downstairs. Her headache was gone but her mind was still a muddle.

She ate dinner in front of the TV. The chatter made

the house feel less empty. She washed her dishes and went back to the den. All her favorite programs were reruns. What to do now? She didn't have a book to read. Maybe answer some letters? Anything to keep her mind off of Peter . . . Deedee . . . Jeremiah . . . Sally.

Jayne fetched paper and pen from Aunt Liz's office and wrote a long, rambling letter to her parents and a couple of short ones to her friends in Palo Alto.

No matter how hard she tried her thoughts always returned to the forbidden list. About Peter and Deedee she could do nothing. But for Sally?

"No way!" she said, and turned the TV up. Later, if anyone had asked her, she couldn't have told them what she had watched.

When the news came on she switched off the TV, turned out the den lights, and went upstairs. The house was enveloped in a hushed, expectant silence.

Jayne sighed. "I'll never rest until I do this!"

Without turning on her light, she walked to the middle of the room. "Sally," she whispered. "Sally, where are you?"

Only silence answered her.

"How can I help if I don't know what to do?"

A cool draft of air blew past her, ruffling the curtains at the window.

Jayne took a few steps toward the window. As she looked out, Jeremiah appeared on the cobblestone sidewalk in front of Bruton Parish Church. He was looking directly up at her! With an imperative wave of his arm, he beckoned her.

Jayne was frozen in place. Did he want her?"

"Go. Please go. Tell him I have confessed at last."

Jayne whirled around but no one was there. She looked back out the window. Jeremiah still waited.

"All right. I'm coming," Jayne said. Almost in a trance, she checked to see if she had her key, closed her door, and walked back downstairs.

She stepped off the back porch into the velvety dark. Robot-like, she walked to the front of the house. Duke of Gloucester Street was deserted . . . except for Jeremiah who stood waiting impatiently, hands on hips.

He waited until she began crossing the street before he slipped into the churchyard.

Jayne broke into a run. "Wait!"

Jeremiah's head popped up behind the brick wall. He motioned her to silence with a finger to his lips.

"Wait. I have a message . . ."

Jeremiah had vanished.

Jayne stood before the wooden gate, shifting from one foot to the other. Caution told her not to enter. Something stronger tugged her forward.

She opened the gate and followed the path to the front of the church. Her heart was beating a hundred miles an hour. She could feel the sweat running down inside her T-shirt.

Jeremiah stood a few yards away. Not on the path. In the cemetery. Among the gravestones. Again, he motioned her to follow.

The first step was the most difficult. She hated to leave the safety of the path. But she'd come too far to chicken out now! Swallowing her fear, she stepped among the dead.

Unlike Jeremiah who flitted effortlessly through the tombstones, she had to pick her way carefully as she followed the soft halo of light surrounding Jeremiah.

Suddenly the light disappeared under the drooping limbs of a giant magnolia tree.

Jayne hesitated, then dodged between the aromatic branches. Darkness enveloped her like a shroud. Her quarry was nowhere to be seen! "Hsst! Up here."

She looked up. Jeremiah perched on a large limb, half-way up the massive tree. "You come down here!" Jayne commanded

"You climb up. 'Tis safer."

"Heights make me dizzy."

"This isn't high," Jeremiah scoffed. "Come on up. Hurry!"

Reluctantly, Jayne obeyed. The tree was easy to climb. Within seconds she was perched on a fat branch opposite Jeremiah.

"Good. We should be safe here," Jeremiah whispered as Jayne fought to control her breathing. "Gad! You do look like Sally!"

"Sally confesses and begs you to forgive her," Jayne said, clutching tightly to the tree after looking down.

"Don't look down. Be quiet and listen. Sally must know what happened."

"All right. Tell me quick."

In a low urgent voice, Jeremiah began. "I carried Sally's message to Colin as I promised. But we had to change the plan. It was too dangerous for Colin to come to Williamsburg. Colin had friends in Baltimore. He gave me money for Sally's passage. 'How will you get through the picket lines?' I asked him. Colin vowed he could do it. But I knew what was in the wind so I gave him my talisman and the code. He could go anywhere with that."

"Weren't you afraid to give safe passage to a Tory?"

"Colin was no Tory! He sympathized with our cause."

"So you gave him your talisman . . ."

"Aye. Then Colin took a ring from his finger. 'This is my family crest,' says he. 'Give it to Sally with my love. I'll meet her in Baltimore.' So I took the ring, the money, and a love note that Colin scribed, and started home.

"I was still behind British lines when I spied someone else form Williamsburg. Yon silky-voiced merchant, Wyatt Saunders, was singing his black heart out to a redcoat captain about our numbers and gun placements."

"Isn't Wyatt Saunders the man who courted Sally?" Jayne asked, wide-eyed.

"Aye. And she refused him."

"What did you do then?"

"Hightailed it back to report that traitor! In my haste I was careless and got caught. Though I gave the code—'Strike a Blow for Freedom'—without my marker I wasn't believed. Especially since I carried a sack of silver. I didn't have time for long explanations. I broke away on foot. I was pursued but they were no match for me! I knew every swamp, field, and path in the area."

"Why were you caught then?" Jayne asked, not liking his cocky manner.

"Bad luck and Wyatt Saunders! Bad luck to be recog nized and worse luck that turncoat Saunders should come along and hear the tale. He joined the pursuit. No fool, he. He rightly thought I might have seen him. He reasoned I would go home and he lay in wait for me."

"But you didn't go home!"

"Nay, I had better sense. I had two missions. One, to get the message and ring to Sally; the other, to expose Mr. Saunders. I left the ring and the note where Sally would be sure to find it. Then I ran for Captain Rawley's. Wyatt shot me in the back as I left the churchyard."

"And you were named the traitor."

"Aye. And Sally never came to fetch her note and ring. I failed in both missions," Jeremiah said sadly.

"What happened to Wyatt Saunders?"

An impish grin lit Jeremiah's face. "Oh, Wyatt figured I'd left something in the churchyard. He thought it was something that would expose him. Old Wyatt became very religious. He spent many hours at this church, yet he never discovered the secret. Even after his death, the scoundrel wouldn't give up and rest in undeserved peace."

Jayne wasn't really listening to Jeremiah. Her thoughts had turned back to Sally. "Where did you hide the ring so Sally would be sure to find it?"

"In the hidey-hole at your feet. Colin and Sally used it to pass love notes. This tree was much smaller then. It was a perfect drop. Everyone came to the church. That's why I've wanted Sally to come here all these years."

Jayne looked down the trunk of the tree. A gnarled hole, no larger than her fist, marred the smooth, shiny tree trunk. "Is it still there?" she whispered.

"Aye. I tucked it in my flint box. Take it to Sally and end her misery. Colin loved her." Then he added diffidently, "And if it is possible, clear the Custis name."

Jayne eased herself down a branch and stuck her hand into the hole. At first she felt nothing but leaves and twigs. She edged closer and rammed her arm in up to her elbow. Her fingers closed around a rough object.

"I've got it!" she yelled, pulling the object free.

"And I have you!" a voice cackled.

A moist, ghostly hand gripped Jayne's ankle, yanking her from her precarious perch.

"Ye'll not ruin my good name, ye fickle wench!" hissed the voice as Jayne tumbled to the ground.

Triumphant laughter was the last sound Jayne heard before the black void swallowed her.

Chapter Ten

Floating . . .

She had passed through the black void. Now she drifted on a sea of pink nothingness. Pain, people, and problems were gone. She felt as if she could float here forever . . . like a child's balloon set free to sail in a bright summer sky.

Only . . . Only someone held her string . . . tugged her back . . . called her name . . .

"Jayne . . . Jayne, can you hear me?"

There was something else, too. Something she had to do . . . something unfinished. . . . She resisted. She didn't want to leave her peaceful haven. It would be too sad . . .

"Jayne."

Jayne opened her tear-wet eyes. Her head throbbed. Through blurred vision, she saw Aunt Liz bending over her. . . . Another figure swam into view . . . the hawk-nosed man from the library . . .

I'm still dreaming, she thought, closing her heavy lids again.

"Jayne, can you see me?"

Jayne fought the pain in her head and the lead weights on her eyes. She forced her eyelids open. "An' L-i-z?" she croaked through stiff, dry lips.

"Thank God! She's conscious," Aunt Liz said, her face wreathed in smiles and relief.

"Yes. Take it easy, Liz. Let her come back gradually," the man said, moistening Jayne's dry lips with a wet cloth.

"Wh-where . . . am . . . I?" Jayne asked, struggling through a red haze of pain.

"In a hospital," the man answered. "You've had a nasty fall. I'm Dr. McNeil. Can you see both of us clearly?"

Jayne blinked several times and their images became less blurred. "Yes."

"Excellent. You may close your eyes now, if you like. Can you still hear me?"

Jayne started to nod but changed her mind when a white-hot pain crashed through her skull. "Y-yes," she gasped. "Which hospital?"

"Don't move your head. You have a concussion. It's going to hurt like bloody hell for a few days. We'll give you something for the pain later."

"Hospital?" Jayne asked desperately.

"Williamsburg General," Aunt Liz answered. "It's a good hospital. Don't worry."

"That's correct, Jayne. Now, just a bit more and we'll let you rest. Can you move your legs?"

Jayne moved first the left leg and then the right. The effort exhausted her.

"Good. How about your arms?"

She raised her left arm easily. The right one seemed frozen. "Can't," she murmured.

"Don't push her, Colin," Aunt Liz warned.

"That's all right, Jayne. You're holding something in your hand. Perhaps if you let it go your arm would move," Dr. McNeil suggested.

"No!" Jayne said loudly. Then she slipped back into unconsciousness. She awoke hearing low voices. She strained to hear the conversation.

"I still feel responsible," Aunt Liz said. "Perhaps my theory was wrong and I gave her too much freedom."

"I'm no child psychologist, but your actions sound proper to me," Dr. McNeil said.

"I still feel guilty for not checking on her when I came in Saturday night."

"A thirteen-year-old doesn't need a nanny," Dr. McNeil responded in his clipped voice. "You had no reason to check her room. Wouldn't have prevented her fall in any case."

Aunt Liz sighed. "I know. But I'd feel much better if I could reach John and Anne. I can't understand John's behavior. When I finally reached his boss, he said John had stomped out of the embassy, after advising him to go jump in the Atlantic!"

Jayne giggled.

Aunt Liz was by her side immediately. "Awake again? How do you feel?"

"Better," Jayne replied. And it was true this time. "Will someone tell me what happened?"

"We thought you might tell us," Aunt Liz said, her voice sharp with worry.

"You had a nasty fall," Dr. McNeil said calmly. "From a tree, evidently. Knocked yourself out. Rector Coatsworth heard you moaning as he went to service Sunday morning. Luckily, he remembered seeing you around your aunt's house. He called her after he called the rescue squad."

Everything came back in a rush. Jayne's face paled and she clutched her right hand more tightly around the object it held. "What day is today?" she asked, stalling for time to collect her wits.

"Monday, the fourth of July," Dr. McNeil answered. "The date the sun began setting on the British Empire."

Jayne recognized the accent now. "You're a Tory!"

"Guilty as charged," Dr. McNeil responded, laughing.

"What has that got to do with anything?" demanded Aunt Liz.

"Let Jayne tell this her way," Dr. McNeil cautioned.

Jayne began hesitantly, "Well, you see, I was sorta into this history stuff. You know, the journals and all. I—uh—came across something I wanted to check out . . . in Bruton Parish churchyard. So, I went over there. Something scared me and I climbed up a tree . . . then I guess I fell out. That's all I remember."

Aunt Liz looked exasperated.

Dr. McNeil looked skeptical.

"Couldn't you have waited until morning?" Aunt Liz asked.

"I could have but I didn't. You know how impulsive I am."

"Your mother mentioned moody and antisocial. She didn't say anything about impulsive," Aunt Liz said, smiling. "It's just as well. I haven't found you to be any of those and nothing would have prepared me for your nightly adventure."

"Mom should have mentioned awkward. Agile people don't fall out of trees. Sometimes my arms and legs don't work together very well."

"It will pass," Dr. McNeil assured her. "You should have seen me at thirteen. I couldn't tie my own shoe-laces."

"Can you now?" Jayne asked slyly.

"I wear slip-ons. Loafers, as you Yanks say." Dr. McNeil responded, straight-faced.

Jayne grinned. She decided she liked Dr. McNeil. Looking at her aunt, she said, "Did Dad really tell Mr. Howard to go jump in the Atlantic?"

"That's what the august Mr. Howard told me."

"Good!" Jayne paused, then said with alarm, "You haven't called them home, have you?"

"I have a call in for them at their next scheduled stop. Of course, if Colin says you are all right, then there's no need for them to rush back."

"Why don't you check with the laboratory for Jayne's latest X-rays, while I give her a quick exam," Dr. McNeil suggested. "Then we'll know for certain."

"I'll do that. Be back shortly," Aunt Liz said, giving Jayne's hand a quick squeeze.

Dr. McNeil listened to her heart, took her pulse, and checked her eyes very quickly. "Now, Jayne, would you care to open your hand?" he asked casually.

Very slowly, she opened her stiffened fingers. A small, crusty tin box dropped on the white coverlet. Her fingers scrabbled to retrieve it.

Dr. McNeil picked it up and put it in her hand.

Jayne looked at the box with awe and relief. Jeremiah's flint box! She hadn't imagined the whole thing.

"Shall I open it for you?"

Jayne swallowed. "Yes . . . please."

Opening the box wasn't easy. The lid was supposed to slide back but it wouldn't budge.

"I'm afraid I shall have to pry it loose. Is that all right?"

"Yes. Yes, please."

Dr. McNeil took out a pocketknife and very carefully pried the lid off. Without looking at the contents, he handed it back to Jayne. "There you are."

The box held a small piece of flint, dust, and a blackish-green ring. Jayne removed the ring carefully. It was a plain ring with a raised, unreadable design as a crest. Tears glistened in her eyes. Oh, how much this would have meant to Sally, if only it had been delivered!

"May I examine it?"

Reluctantly, Jayne handed it to him.

"Hmm. Very interesting. Not worth much as a treasure trove, I expect."

"It's worth a lot to someone!" Jayne shot back. She extended her hand for the ring. "Uh . . . Could we keep this between us? Just for a little while. I have to show it to someone before everyone makes a big deal out of it."

Unexpectedly, Dr. McNeil smiled. "Right. Mum's the word."

Before she could say thank you, Aunt Liz came back.

For the first time Jayne noticed how tired she looked. "Jayne's X-rays are fine. I called Lavina while I was out, too. She sends her love and wants you to hurry home."

"When can I go?" Jayne asked anxiously, clutching the flint box.

"Dr. Trumka, that's your admitting physician, and I would like you to stay one more night. Just to ensure you remain quiet for another twelve hours or so," Dr. McNeil replied.

"All right. You both look as if you could use some rest yourselves."

"We're fine," Aunt Liz said. "You sleep now. I'll be right here."

"Nonsense, Liz!" Dr. McNeil said. "You're going home. The nurses can take care of Jayne. Don't be foolish."

After a few protests Aunt Liz agreed.

"I'll look in on you later, Jayne," Dr. McNeil said.

Aunt Liz kissed her cheek. "You are very fortunate, Jayne. Your concussion isn't severe, but if it had been, you'd have had the best neurosurgeon in the world to help you. Isn't it lucky Dr. McNeil was right here in Williamsburg? Get some rest now."

"I will if you promise not to come back until morning. Lavina doesn't need two patients to take care of."

"It's a deal," Aunt Liz said, smiling.

Jayne slept most of the day . . . when the nurses would let her. It seemed as if someone woke her every ten minutes to check her temperature, her pulse, or her blood pressure.

An overseas call interrupted her dinner. Her father's

voice, sounding unnaturally high, came through loud and clear. "Jayne, what happened? Are you truly all right?"

"I fell out of a tree. I'm okay, Dad. Honest. I have a whopper of a headache but otherwise I'm fine."

"I think I'm going to want to hear more about this tree," her father said, sounding more normal. "I'm sure you'll have a good story for us when we return."

"Sure I will . . . if you don't come home too soon. I want to hear your story, too. You know, how you told Mr. Howard to go jump in the Atlantic. He was long overdue for a swim, in my opinion."

"Right you are, Jayne. Your mother and I made a terrible mistake. We allowed these government types to intimidate us. We've been running from pillar to post like beggars instead of educators. We were fed up with all of the Mickey Mouse meetings and . . . Here, your mother wants to speak with you. I love you."

"We're coming home," Mrs. Custis announced. "We're taking the first flight available."

"Mom, I'm okay. Please don't screw up your chances now."

"Jayne, you're far more important that any language program. Americans have managed to get along for years speaking only English. We, however, can't get along without you."

Her mother's love and concern came through the transatlantic lines much as Elizabeth's had come through in the journal. Something clicked in Jayne's mind. She swallowed the sudden lump in her throat. "Mom, honest, I'm fine. The bump on the head may even have knocked some sense into me."

"What do you mean, Jayne?"

"I did something stupid at Stuart Hill. I was afraid to tell you and Dad because I thought you wouldn't love me anymore. I guess I kinda wigged out."

"Oh, Jayne! Don't you know that no matter what you do or how you behave, we'll always love you?"

"I do now."

There was a small silence on the line. Then her mother said, "Well, I never thought I'd be grateful for a bump on the head, but I am. Are you certain you're all right now?"

"Absolutely. Positively. And I promise not to climb any more trees, act stupid, or give Aunt Liz any more trouble. Honest."

"I believe you . . . mainly because you sound like our old Jayne again. Please take care of yourself. We may not say it often enough, but we do love you."

Jayne breathed a satisfied sigh. "I know, Mom. I love you, too. See ya next month. 'Bye now."

It took Jayne a few minutes to realize her mother hadn't even asked what stupid thing she'd done at Stuart Hill. Nothing could have reassured her more. Now she wondered why she'd ever doubted her parents' love.

"Maybe that's an unpleasant part of growing up," she mumbled before she dozed off.

Dr. Trumka came in later and gave her a brief examination. He said she was allowed to get out of bed and go to the bathroom, if a nurse was present for the first few times.

Aunt Liz and Lavina called. And, just as visiting hours were over, Dr. McNeil walked in.

Shutting the door firmly behind him, he said, "I believe we should talk, Jayne."

Jayne had a feeling Dr. McNeil would want to talk, especially since he had a name like Colin. . . .

Chapter Eleven

"Do you mind?" Dr. McNeil asked, holding out his pipe.

"No, I like it. My dad smokes a pipe."

"Isn't good for either of us. But I think better with a pipe in my mouth. Now, Jayne, I've come to tell you a bedtime story."

Jayne smiled at the thought of this dignified, proper Englishman telling bedtime stories. "I don't think I'm too old for that. Go ahead."

Dr. McNeil folded himself into a chair and took a deep puff of his pipe, filling the room with honey-sweet aroma. "In seventeen hundred and nine, Queen Anne gave lands on the River York in the Virginia Colony to Laird Robert Bruce McNeil . . . presumably for some service to the Crown. Laird McNeil sent his second son, Bruce, to develop the estate. Later Bruce brought his wife and children over. River Bend prospered. Bruce eventually returned to England, leaving his son William to manage his holdings. William Bruce McNeil and his two sons were at River Bend in 1776 when the Colonies broke away from England. They chose to remain here during the war, having some feelings for both sides. By war's end, William had returned to England to become Laird McNeil. Robert, the eldest son, was holding River Bend for the Crown. And Colin, the youngest son, had disappeared.

"River Bend was confiscated as Tory property and Robert was sent packing. He died on the voyage home. Young Colin finally arrived in England a very bitter man. After his father's death, he became Laird McNeil. By all accounts, he was a cantankerous curmudgeon who hated women and only married because it was his duty. The only thing he disliked more than women was America, or anything American. This crusty ancestor of mine kept only one memento from his American years. This silver coin."

Jayne's heart beat a wild tattoo in her chest when Dr. McNeil held up a silver disk. She wanted to grab it and examine it but she made herself say calmly, "Colin sounds very bitter. I wonder why?"

"That interested me also. He said in his diary that the coin was to remind him of the nature of all Americans. They had confiscated his money, his honor, his land, and his heart."

"Wow! That's a pretty big load of hate."

"I agree. A man would have to have a reason for feeling that strongly. Liz told you that I'm a neurosurgeon. I'm also a genealogist, amateur, to be sure. We British are very family-conscious, you know. When this opportunity as an exchange surgeon came along I accepted readily. I thought it would give me an opportunity to research my family's Colonial history. I must confess I wasn't having much luck researching the coin until you dashed out of the library the other day."

"Oh?"

"Yes. I wondered what had excited you so. I picked up the volume you had been reading. Lo and behold! There was an illustration of my silver coin."

"My coin," Jayne corrected. "It belonged to my ancestor, Jeremiah Custis."

"Fair enough. You have my family signet ring. Would you care to tell me how this came about?"

"I don't think I can. I mean, I can tell you what happened. But not how I know . . . not exactly."

"I would be very interested to hear whatever you can tell me," Dr. McNeil replied. "Being a genealogist is akin to being a detective. I'd like to solve this mystery."

"So would I," Jayne said, and began. At first she chose her words very carefully, pretending to have learned everything from the old journal. But she soon became caught up in the story and several "Sally saids" and "Jeremiah saids" slipped in.

"I see," murmured Dr. McNeil when she finished. "It's a sad, true story of war-crossed lovers."

"Can I keep the ring for a little while? There's something I need to do with it."

Dr. McNeil reached into his pocket. "Here, take the coin, too. It will help."

"I wish I had the note," Jayne said absently, turning the coin over in her palm.

"Paper deteriorates over the years. Sally will believe you without it."

Jayne's mouth fell open.

Dr. McNeil's face was expressionless. Only his eyes acknowledged their secret. "Liz tells me you are a great reader," he said calmly. "Have you perchance read any Shakespeare?"

Jayne was so amazed she forgot and shook her head. A pain skyrocketed through her head as a reminder.

Dr. McNeil was by her bedside quickly. "Easy now, young lady. No sudden movements." Then, correctly interpreting her expression, he continued, "You might like the Bard, Jayne. Take *Hamlet,* for example. Prince Hamlet is talking with his father's ghost in one scene. Hamlet's friend, Horatio, can't believe his ears. Hamlet says to him, 'There are more things in heaven and earth, Horatio, than are dreamt of in our philosophy.' And Hamlet was right, you know. We don't have a scientific explanation for everything. Many intelligent, rational people have encountered spirits. So don't worry about what you have experienced. Accept it and do what you must. Good night, Jayne. Sleep well."

"Good night, Dr. McNeil," Jayne said, "and thank you." She felt as if a great weight had been lifted from her. She wasn't crazy. Dr. McNeil, a man of science, believed her. She was certain Aunt Liz would never have bought such a weird tale.

She took a deep breath of the pipe-scented air. For the first time she felt an enormous sense of pride in Jeremiah. Instead of being a traitor, he was really a hero! Even though he was just a kid, he'd played a part in the

94

struggle for independence. She understood why some people were family-proud. Count Martha Jayne Custis among them now.

Jayne could hardly wait to get back and show the ring and talisman to Sally. Sally had been wrong about a lot of things. No wonder she hadn't rested easy.

Fourth of July fireworks lit the night sky, making beautiful, silent patterns outside her window.

Jayne watched the display, smiling. She couldn't take part in today's celebration but tomorrow she would celebrate a special day of freedom with Sally and Jeremiah.

Chapter Twelve

Homecoming. Never had she been so happy to be anywhere. The little blue room looked heavenly. Smelled heavenly, too.

"I got your lunch all ready," Lavina said, fluffing Jayne's pillows. "Sticky buns for dessert."

"I smelled them when I came in. I think I could eat a dozen. Hospital food is enough to make you sick," Jayne said.

"I quite agree," Dr. McNeil said. "I believe they plan it that way to keep you longer."

"Colin!"

"It's true, Liz. Admit it," Dr. McNeil said, smiling at Aunt Liz's surprise.

"You-all go argue somewhere else," Lavina ordered. "This child needs her rest."

Meekly, both doctors left.

"Now, I'm gonna bring up your lunch before that boy comes pounding at the door again," Lavina said.

"What boy?"

"Just how many boyfriends do you have in Williamsburg?"

"None!"

"Well, you could have fooled me! Peter has been camped on our doorstep for two days now. I told him to come back after lunch."

"I don't want to see him."

"Hah!" Lavina snorted and walked out.

When Lavina came back to pick up Jayne's tray she brought the mail and Peter with her.

"Hi," Peter said. "You look pretty good for someone with a cracked skull."

"I'm fine, thank you. You can go now."

Peter's blue eyes looked puzzled. "What's wrong?"

Jayne met his gaze without flinching. "The bump on my head isn't any reason for you to be nice to me. So good-bye."

"What the heck are you talking about?"

Jayne sighed. "Look, Peter, I know you were just killing time with me until Blondie came home. I don't blame you. She's a real fox."

"What blondie? What are you babbling about? Are you mad because I went to Charlottesville? I didn't want to go. I thought I explained that in my letter."

"What letter? I didn't get any letter. But you better believe I got the message."

Peter sank onto a chair. "Look, I know I can't hear, but somehow I'm not even reading you right. Let's start where we left off last Thursday night. Okay?"

Some of what Peter had said was beginning to sink in. Something about going to Charlottesville . . . "Okay."

"Right," Peter said, brushing his hair from his eyes. "You know Dad called for me? Okay. He was all excited about this German otologist who was visiting the University of Virginia Medical Center. Dr. Swartzloff had agreed to examine me if we could get to Charlottesville by eight o'clock on Friday morning. Dad and I argued for hours about it. I didn't want to see another lousy doctor. Dad said it was worth a chance. Dad won. He always wins. By that time it was too late for him to call you for me. So I wrote you a letter. I stuck it out for the mailman when we left at six that morning. End of story."

"What did this doctor tell you?"

"Later. You tell your story now," Peter said firmly.

"Well, I hung around all day waiting for you. When you didn't show, I rode over to your house. This gorgeous blonde model-type was coming out your door. We—uh-had some words. At least, she did. What it boiled down to was that, now she was home, I could go play in my sandbox."

"And you believed her?"

Jayne blushed. "Well, I saw your bike. I thought you were . . . uh . . ."

"Chicken," Peter finished for her.

"Not exactly. I thought after you found out what kind of person I was, you didn't want to have anything to do with me."

"I don't believe this!" Peter said, shaking his head. "I thought you knew me better."

"I've only known you a few weeks! What was I supposed to think? Why was she in your house? She acted like you were her property," Jayne yelled. It made her head hurt abominably.

For some reason, Peter smiled!

"Her name is Deedee Darlington. She's my next-door neighbor. Dad asked the Darlingtons to bring in our mail. Deedee's an airhead. Would you believe the only reason she likes me is, and I quote, 'We look so good together.' I choose my friends for different reasons. And it's not because they're perfect. Everyone makes mistakes."

"Yeah, even adults," Jayne said, smiling.

"Well, now that that's settled, go on with your story," urged Peter.

"There isn't much else to tell. Saturday was sort of a topsy-turvy day. I ended up staying home alone. I saw that boy again and decided to follow him . . ."

"You went back in the cemetery at night?"

"Yeah. But while I was poking around I heard something that scared me. So I climbed a tree . . . and fell out. End of story."

Peter was still looking at her with astonishment. "I can't believe you went back! You were shaking like a leaf when we came out of there."

"Believe it!" Jayne said, touching the bandage on her head.

"Did you think it was a bear?" Peter asked, grinning. "I've heard people climb trees to get away from them."

Jayne wasn't ready to confide in Peter . . . yet. "I don't know what I thought. All I know is that I've climbed my last tree!"

"I certainly hope so," Aunt Liz said from the doorway.

"Peter, I hate to be an old meanie, but I think Jayne should rest now."

"Sure, Dr. Custis. I'll come back tomorrow, if that's okay?" he said, looking straight at Jayne.

Jayne flushed with pleasure. "Sure. We didn't finish our chess game, you know."

"Right," Peter said, and started out.

Jayne grabbed his hand. "Wait. You didn't tell me what the doctor said."

Peter shrugged. "Good news and bad news. The good news is, they're working on a new implant technique and I'm a good candidate. The bad news is, I can't even consider the operation until I'm eighteen. And even then there's no guarantee of success."

"I'm sorry, Peter."

"Don't be. I'm learning to live with it. Dad can't."

"He only wants to help you."

Peter flashed a smile. "I know. Hey, you're a funny one to be defending parents."

"Shhh! Don't tell anyone, but I think I'm beginning to understand them." She let go of Peter's hand but not before Peter gave hers a comforting squeeze.

"Catch you later, partner," he said.

"It won't be too difficult. I'm not going anywhere."

The warm glow left by Peter's visit lasted long after he had gone. By evening she was tired of Lavina, Aunt Liz, and Dr. McNeil popping in and out of her room, asking how she felt. She wanted to tell them she felt as well as could be expected for someone with a knot on her head the size of a hen's egg. Instead, she smiled and answered politely. She knew she'd really feel lots better if she could get one more thing settled.

The house wasn't quiet until almost midnight. When she hadn't heard a sound for a half hour, Jayne eased herself out of bed. She removed the coin, the ring, and the battered flint box from under her pillow and hobbled toward the moonlit window. Placing her treasures on the table beside the journal, she sank onto a chair calling softly, "Sally . . . Sally, where are you?"

The moonbeams became a mist and the mist became Sally. "What happened to you? Did Jeremiah do this?" Sally asked, wringing her hands.

"No! It wasn't Jeremiah. He loves you. All these years he's been trying to make you understand what happened. But you wouldn't come to the churchyard."

Sally hung her head. "I could not. Even without my oath, I could not. I could not face Jeremiah."

"Then just listen while I tell you what really happened that night." In a low voice she began, interrupted by gasps of pleasure and woe from Sally. When she reached the part about Wyatt Saunders, Sally was beside herself with fury.

"That mealymouthed traitor! I knew he was no good, though Mama favored him. And to think he is buried with honor in Bruton Parish churchyard!"

"If it's any comfort, Wyatt Saunders has not been resting in peace," Jayne said.

"Nor should he ever!"

Jayne pointed to the ring. "This is the ring Colin sent to you. Do you recognize it?"

Sally took the ring and caressed it with her fingers.

The blackish patina disappeared and the golden ring glistened in the moonlight. "Aye. 'Tis Colin's. It is his family's seal."

"He meant it for you," Jayne said softly. "But now another Colin McNeil has come to collect his family heirloom. Shall I give it to him?"

Sally replaced the ring on the table. "Yes. All that matters is that my Colin loved me. I do not need the ring."

"I'll keep the talisman with the journals. So that from now on everyone will know that Jeremiah really was one of Rawley's Runners," Jayne promised.

Sally smiled. "You are a true kinswoman, Jayne Custis. My spirit will rest now. Thanks be to you," she said as her form began to fade.

Jayne watched in silence as the mist dissolved back into moonlight. The room felt empty . . . even a little lonely. She sighed and gathered up her treasures.

Dr. Colin McNeil could have his signet ring back now. She would keep the silver talisman. Perhaps someday she would even write a story about it.

Glancing out the window, she saw Jeremiah standing across the street in his usual place. He was looking up at the window. Jayne held up the silver talisman and the gold ring.

With a flourish, Jeremiah removed his tricorn hat and bowed deeply. Then he, too, vanished.

Tears glistened on Jayne's cheek. "Good-bye, Jeremiah. Good-bye, Sally," she whispered.

Feeling half happy, half sad, Jayne started back to bed but decided to visit the bathroom first. She eased open her door and tiptoed across the dark hall.

"Jayne?"

"Just making a necessary trip, Aunt Liz."

"Oh," Aunt Liz said, turning on her lamp. "For a moment I thought you were a ghost."

"I thought you didn't believe in spirits," Jayne teased.

Her aunt looked at her sternly. "It was only a manner of speaking, Jayne. Of course there are no such things as ghosts!"

Jayne chuckled all the way to the necessary. Aunt Liz was protesting too much. Sally had been more effective than she knew.

HOWLING GOOD FUN
FROM AVON CAMELOT

WEREWOLF, COME HOME   75908-X/$2.75 US/$3.25 CAN

HOW TO BE A VAMPIRE IN ONE EASY LESSON
75906-3/$2.75 US/$3.25 CAN

ISLAND OF THE WEIRD   75907-1/$2.75 US/$3.25 CAN

THE MONSTER IN CREEPS HEAD BAY
75905-5/$2.75 US/$3.25 CAN

THINGS THAT GO BARK IN THE PARK
75786-9/$2.75 US/$3.25 CAN

YUCKERS!   75787-7/$2.75 US/$3.25 CAN

M IS FOR MONSTER   75423-1/$2.75 US/$3.25 CAN

BORN TO HOWL   75425-8/$2.50 US/$3.25 CAN

THERE'S A BATWING IN MY LUNCHBOX
75426-6/$2.75 US/$3.25 CAN

THE PET OF FRANKENSTEIN 75185-2/$2.50 US/$3.25 CAN

Z IS FOR ZOMBIE   75686-2/$2.75 US/$3.25 CAN

MONSTER MASHERS   75785-0/$2.75 US/$3.25 CAN